THE LIGH
CODE

Ellie Booton's Journal, No. 2

Hello! I hope you enjoy this book.
Flinty Maguire

flinty maguire

Burdock House

Published by Burdock House

www.burdockhouse.co.uk

info@burdockhouse.co.uk

First edition paperback published 2015

Text © Flinty Maguire, 2015

Illustrations © Flinty Maguire, 2015

Printed in the UK by The Printing House,

3rd Floor, 14 Hanover Street, London, W1S 1YH

British Library Cataloguing in Publication Data

A CIP catalogue record for this book is available from

the British Library

ISBN: 978-0-9930984-0-6

For Elizabeth

By Flinty Maguire

Trouble at the Crab Shack Café
Ellie Booton's Journal, No. 1
Also available on Kindle

The Lighthouse Code
Ellie Booton's Journal, No. 2
Also available on Kindle

In this book you'll see an occasional asterisk *
This means there's an extra jot at the back.

For more information about Flinty Maguire

www.burdockhouse.co.uk

Grateful thanks to Patrick Reynolds
and James Duncan

Special thanks to my grandson, Jack,
for testing this book.

A great mystery making you want to
flick to the last page.

- *Jack Lockwood*

The first red flash

Everything feels a bit strange. The weather is awful, it wakes me up. I climb out of bed and curl up on the window seat. Dogs have very good hearing and even with the wind howling outside, Herman pads up the stairs to see who's awake. I hear him sniff at my door so I let him in and he sits by me for a while, his head in my lap. It's inky-black outside but when the lighthouse beam sweeps round, I see waves crashing on the beach.

Herman belly-crawls under my bunk and falls asleep. I'm just about to go back to bed when I see something odd. Below the rotating lighthouse beam, there's a red flash of light. It disappears and I wonder if I've seen it at all. I climb into bed and listen to the wind, and to Herman quietly snoring.

The Pavarotti principle

We're not quite an ideal family. I sit at the kitchen table eating Rice Krispies. Grandma sips coffee and reads The Independent. Eddie, my big brother, who works with Grandma making sculptures and what they call objects d'art, is crunching Corn Flakes and slurping tea. He makes disgusting noises but doesn't speak. Eddie is not a morning person – and sometimes he's not an afternoon or an evening person either.

Dad has finally fixed the whiteboard on the kitchen wall and we all scribble stuff on it, though Dad uses it the most because he's a writer and it helps him organise his thoughts.

He scrawls: 'I might be a Pavarotti.'*

I MIGHT BE A PAVAROTTI

'What's a Pavarotti?' I ask. It sounds like an animal disease.

Dad says, 'Not what. *Who!* Pavarotti was the world's greatest opera singer.'

I pull a face. 'Singing's not for you, Dad.'

When Dad sings, wolves howl in sympathy.

2

Dad says, 'The point is, Pavarotti discovered he was a great singer just by singing. You don't know how good you're going to be at something until you've tried.'

Eddie scratches his head. It's been a while, I think, since his hair saw a comb.

'Or how useless,' he says.

'OK, I'm not a great singer' - Eddie snorts - 'but this isn't about singing. It's about this next b-blithering book.' He chews his lower lip. 'I've never tackled a project like this before. What if I've bitten off more than I can chew?'

Oh no. Here we go again. Dad's been banging on about this book for weeks and we're all sick to the back teeth of it. The thing is – this is Dad's BIG CHANCE. Dad is a ghost writer, so he writes stories for other people but NEVER gets his name printed on the book. But this time, he's been asked to write the biography of a young up-and-coming opera singer who might, one day, be famous - though I wouldn't bet on it. Dad's name will be printed on the *front* cover, so when this Watford Warbler (as I call him) finally makes it BIG, the book might make Dad a bit famous too. Dad likes to think he's a pretty relaxed guy, but this book has got him very ANXIOUS and TWITCHY.

Mum comes in and starts to load the dishwasher. She looks at the whiteboard and sighs. 'You don't have to be Pavarotti to sing a decent song,' she mutters.

'I'll sort the dishwasher out, Flora,' says Grandma.

'No Ruby,' says Mum, firmly. 'It's not your turn. It's Walter's turn but he's too busy worrying about being... *great.*'

Mum sounds *really* fed up.

My mum doesn't like:

1. Loading the dishwasher, especially when there's gravy dripping off the plates.
2. Picking up pants from the floor (or other items of laundry).
3. My dad.

That's right. I've noticed it lately and I'm not sure whether it's a permanent or a temporary thing. They snap at one another – and I suppose that's why things feel strange. It's hard to feel happy and relaxed when your parents aren't getting along.

There are plenty of people living in this house. When Grandpa died, my family came to live with Grandma so she wouldn't be lonely. The house must be magnetic because a few weeks ago, Nanna and Gramps (Mum's parents) came to live here too. Gramps is a very fussy eater and sometimes he falls - and when Gramps falls, believe me, it takes more than one person to pick him up. So now, Grandma's house is jam-packed with Mum and Dad, Eddie, Fin (my sticky little brother), and me – *and now* Nanna and Gramps. Grandma says she can't complain of *ever* feeling lonely now, though sometimes she wishes she could. There's also Herman, Grandma's Labrador and Eliza, our cat, who spends most of her time on Dad's knee or asleep on a chair in his office. And even though cats are meant to calm you down, Dad is

FRACTIOUS – which sounds a bit like FRACTIONS – a good word, because he's not a simple whole any more – he's something irritating like **seven-ninths.**

I say quietly to Mum, 'I've decided to audition for the school musical.'

Dad looks at me over his glasses and says, 'Haven't I always told you - avoid being famous at all costs?'

Dad has always said he *never* wants to be famous because all your tricky moments (like slipping on a banana skin) end up on YouTube.

Mum says, 'Oh, for goodness sake, Walter. It's a school play, not the X Factor.'

'Don't worry, Dad,' I say. 'There's no danger of *you* becoming famous. The Watford Warbler is no one to get excited about.'

And, can you believe it – Dad looks annoyed! I don't get it! He should be relieved.

Let me tell you about the Watford Warbler. He doesn't even sing in English! People have to pretend they understand his songs. Put it this way, it's not the sort of music anyone I know would spend their pocket money on.

Susannah's music on the other hand, is FAB! Susannah is Eddie's girlfriend, though sometimes they're not friends - but when this happens, it's *always* Eddie's fault.

On Monday and Friday Susannah gives me a guitar lesson. We sit in the den and she shows me chords and how to strum. So far, I know A, E and D and there are *loads* of tunes you can play with just three chords. Susannah sings and when I have to change chords, she waits until my fingers are in the right place, then she sings the next bit until I have to change chords again. Susannah says I'm doing well. Sometimes my best friend, Elsie, sits with us and sings along too. It sounds really good. When I know a few more chords, I think I'll play in front of people. I'm starting to think that I can't *avoid* becoming a little bit famous, so there's no harm in auditioning for the school play.

I sit at my desk in school. My form teacher is called Miss Askew (pronounced *ask-you*) which is a very good name for her because she fixes you with her black button eyes that never blink and tilts her head askew, (*a-skew*) when she asks a question. I always think I should give her a biscuit because Herman tilts his head like this when he wants a treat.

Miss Askew loves the colour beige. Her clothes and shoes are beige, and her face. When she puts her hand on her hip she looks like a big beige jug.

The thing is – this play is a *big deal* because Miss Askew (who always produces the school play) – is leaving our school, but nobody knows why. She's a bit old fashioned but I don't think she's *old* as in - *ready to draw her pension.* So this will be her last production and she wants it to be *great!* And that's why she's letting the younger kids audition because, she says, talent has nothing to do with age and she needs to cherry-pick the best.

I want Elsie to audition too, but she's not keen.

Elsie's reasons for not wanting to audition:

6

1. Some kids make fun of her because she has freckles and red curly hair, and she doesn't want to be in the school play in case more kids call her names.

(I understand this. Instead of Ellie, some kids call me Smelly. My surname is Booton – so I'm known as Smelly Boots, which makes me feel a bit FRACTIOUS.)

2. Rehearsals are after school, and Elsie likes to check that her mum is OK as soon as school finishes.

(Elsie's mum, Cadence, owns the Box Brownie café and if the café is quiet, she gets stressed. When parents get stressed, bad things can happen, so most kids try to keep their parents calm if they can.)

3. Elsie doesn't think she has any talent, so there's no point auditioning anyway.

(So NOT TRUE, but she won't believe me, even though I DON'T LIE.)

Grandma says Elsie lacks confidence.

A little bit about CONFIDENCE

CONFIDENCE is belief that you can do something, but if you think confidence is a straightforward thing, think again. Sometimes people believe they can do something well, when they really *can't*. This is called **MISPLACED CONFIDENCE.** I mean, when Eddie was learning to drive, he was sure it would be easy. On his first lesson he parked Dad's car on top of someone's prize butter beans, but only after he'd run over their potato patch, squashed a bucket and smashed their garden fence.

You can also be **OVER-CONFIDENT** – which means that you might be good at something, but not as good as you think you are – and it can be a **big shock** to find that out. For example, you might be able to juggle three tennis balls and think that juggling three tins of beans is just as easy - until you miss, get hit on the head and end up in hospital with a big concussion.

And then there's **LACK OF CONFIDENCE**, when you might be good at something, but for all sorts of reasons, you just can't or won't believe in yourself.

Confidence is *very tricky.*

I ask Elsie to come to the audition with me because I'm not sure whether I should be confident or not. She agrees, but only because she owes me a favour or two. The one good thing is that the auditions are in the hall, and the only people who hear you sing are Miss Askew and Lara Jeffreys, who is in Year 10. We wait outside the hall until Lara calls our names.

Miss Askew says, 'When you're ready girls.'

My legs feel like jelly.

I count us in, 'One, two, three,' and we start our song, *Over The Rainbow.**

Miss Askew interrupts us after the first verse and says, 'Very nice, Elsie. Good effort, Ellie. Thank you.'

She whispers to Lara who writes something down on a clipboard. Elsie and I hurry out for a quick walk round the playground.

Elsie says, 'That was scary.'

I say, 'It's called stage fright and you can take tablets for it, I think. But it's good to face your fears - sometimes anyway. It might not be a good idea to go up to a ferocious, wild animal and introduce yourself.'

Elsie says, 'Especially at mealtime.'

We laugh, but I know what Elsie means. It is scary on the stage, and if that's how it feels with just Miss Askew and Lara watching, what will it be like with the hall *full* of people, all looking and waiting for me to trip, or forget my lines or something?

Anyway, I have to wait a few days to hear if I've been chosen, and in the meantime I can persuade myself and Elsie that the school play will be heaps of fun.

PS and the letter L

It's already gloomy when we stop by the Box Brownie café after school. There are twinkle lights around the windows and a line of seagulls on the roof hoping there will be scraps for supper. Inside, there's lots of happy chatter. Swing music plays softly on the jukebox and there's a smell of vanilla, coffee and cake. Elsie's mum seems happy, so we climb the hill to my house to do our homework. Eddie sits at the kitchen table with his laptop, updating the website which sells the things that he and Grandma make in the workshop.

Eddie says, 'Hi Melly Moo. Do you want to check your emails?'

He gets up and I sit down. There's an email from Jack, who visits our town in school holidays. He loves photography and his great-grandma once owned the Box Brownie café, though it was called the Carnation Café then.

FROM: Jack Bell
TO: Menella Booton
SUBJECT: Hi!

Hi Ellie,
Thanks for your email. Sorry it's taken me ages to reply.

I've been busy taking photographs and I've entered one in a magazine competition. If it wins, it will be included in a book. Hope you and Elsie are OK. Say hi to everyone for me.

Jack

There's *no way* I'm going to wait *two whole weeks* before I write back, so I click 'reply' and type:

Hi Jack,

C'est moi, Ellie. I hope your photograph wins. Elsie and I auditioned for the school play today. It's a musical and I hope I get a part. My guitar lessons are going well and I already know 3 chords. Elsie says bonjour, and now we both say au revoir.

PS Are you coming to stay with your Auntie Maggie again? Quand viendras-tu?

The PS is *very important* when you want someone to respond, especially if it's a boy (because boys can be *hideous* at making the effort to stay in touch). I know this because when Eddie went to Art College, Mum once sent him three emails, seven texts and left two voice mail messages, asking what he'd like for his birthday – and he didn't reply to *any* of them. So Mum sent him underpants. Big, baggy grey ones. After that, Eddie made the effort to tell Mum what he *really* wanted for his birthday – and funnily enough, he's NEVER asked for baggy underpants. Mum says that some people have to be *trained* to meet you halfway, because it doesn't always come naturally. So I figure, asking Jack questions is a way of *training* him to write back and throwing in a bit of French adds a bit of sophistication.

Grandma comes in from the workshop and says, 'Hello girls. How was your audition?'

'Awful,' says Elsie.

I say, 'I think we sang really well, actually. We'll get used to being on stage, won't we Grandma?'

Grandma shrugs. 'I don't know, Ellie. It's not something I've ever done.'

And this is surprising, because Grandma is quite old and she usually has the answer to *everything*.

Eddie says, 'Have you got a part in the play then?'

I say, 'We don't know yet.'

Eddie frowns and says, 'Don't count your chickens then.'

But I think I've got a good chance, because I'm learning to play the guitar and Miss Askew wants musical people.

It's a cold, starry night. I'm awake because there's a lot to think about. I wonder if it will make Mum and Dad happy if I get a part in the play. From my window, I can see the Box Brownie café and when Elsie's there, we wave at one another - but it's deserted and in darkness. The lighthouse sweeps its icy light round and round. And then, below the lighthouse beam, a red light appears. Then it goes off - and it comes back on, but it looks like a letter – a bright red L. For a few moments, it's a strong, steady glow. Then it disappears.

Drifting away

It's nearly home time.

Miss Askew says, 'Pay attention, class. I want to tell you about the musical. It's completely *new* and it's never been performed before.'

And I would say most of us in the class are pretty impressed by this news. Will there be a red carpet and photographers on the first night? That's what happens at world premieres, isn't it?

Miss Askew says, 'It's a play wot I wrote,' and she laughs.

We don't get the joke.

'That's what Ernie Wise* used to say,' she says, laughing some more.

I know who he is, so I manage a chuckle, but I'm starting to feel a bit worried.

Miss Askew rolls her eyes, does her jug impression and says, 'Good grief! Look him up on Google, for goodness sake.'

Elsie frowns. She's thinking the same thing as me: *Miss Askew, with her tweed skirts and her big beige cardigans, isn't exactly the most exciting woman in town – so her musical might be... a little bit... BORING.* And if it's boring,

I don't think I want to be in it - so what do I do when she offers me a part?

She says, 'Thank you to everyone who auditioned. I was looking for good, clear singing voices that would reach the back of the hall. I can tell you that the leading lady, Clara, is in *this* class.'

Everyone starts looking round, wondering who it could be. I start to drift away...

I imagine myself as Clara in a long tweed skirt and a sloppy beige cardigan. I trip and slide off the stage, head first, and land in the orchestra pit, in Billy Grogan's tuba. I suddenly feel a bit *sick.*

Miss Askew says, '- and each leading character will have an understudy.'

Juna Budd puts her hand up and asks what an understudy is. Miss Askew looks surprised because it's unusual for Juna to ask a question, or even to speak.

Let me tell you something. I was once an understudy and it's a *very* tricky business. An understudy learns the part of a character and is ready to go on stage if the proper actor, for some reason, can't perform on the night. You want to have a crack at the part, so you start hoping they will trip and twist their ankle - or they'll catch a contagious disease that will take them down - but not kill them, obviously. Being an understudy sort of brings out the worst in people.

I'm thinking this when, suddenly, Elsie grabs my arm and looks a bit pleased and a bit terrified and her eyes are as round as saucers.

I think: *I've got the part! I'm Clara! OH NO!*

Everyone is looking at us, because she's flapping like a fish.

I sort of reel her in a bit and say, 'It's all right,' because that's a good, standard thing to say when you're not sure what's going on.

I tune back into Miss Askew, who is saying '- so Elsie will make an excellent Clara, and Abigail Jennings from Year 9, will be her understudy.'

Suddenly I feel really HOT and CONFUSED. I think: *WHAT?!*

I look at Elsie. She's *pleased!* HOW CAN SHE BE PLEASED? Elsie didn't even want to audition! I definitely don't feel good inside.

I see Miss Askew's mouth moving, but there's no sound except GLUG, GLUG, like she's underwater. And what's worse, lots of chorus parts are given out – GLUG, GLUG - but there's absolutely – GLUG, GLUG – no mention of *my* name. Not... at... all. It's like *I don't exist!*

When school is over, Juna Budd, who's been chosen to be a waif and stray, comes over to Elsie. Juna hardly speaks to anyone, but she says she will walk home with us, even though she lives on the other side of town. When we get to the Box Brownie, I say I have to go straight home for my guitar lesson, even though I don't have one tonight.

Elsie doesn't seem to care. She says, 'OK, Ellie. I'll see you tomorrow,' and she goes inside the café with Juna.

I say, 'Sure,' and pull my mouth into the shape of a smile.

A slippery slope and (the letter) i

Grandma sits at the kitchen table looking glum, which is very unusual because Grandma is normally a smiley person.

I say, 'What's wrong Grandma?'

Grandma sighs, 'It's just one of those days, Ellie, though I'm glad to see you. Have you had a good day?'

I shake my head. I tell Grandma about Miss Askew's play, and how Elsie got the main part and that Abigail Jennings is her understudy.

Grandma says, 'Awkward!'

Just let me explain about Abigail – she is *not* quite a nice girl. She's a bit LIGHT-FINGERED (she once stole something from the Box Brownie café) – and that should surprise you, because her dad is a policeman.

Grandma says, 'Have you got a part in the play?'

I shake my head. Suddenly, I feel hot again, and I burst into tears.

Grandma gives me a hug and pours me a glass of Cherry Good.

She says, 'You're disappointed.'

I nod miserably. I thought I'd get the part because I'm learning to play the guitar and it was *my* idea to audition in the first place. And, truthfully, I'm a bit cross too – Elsie

16

didn't even want to be in the play. And Abigail is Elsie's understudy??? *PUR-LEASE!* And now, Juna Budd wants to hang around Elsie, and I've always had the feeling that Juna doesn't like me.

So where does that leave me?

On the outside – that's where! I feel HORRIBLE.

Grandma looks at me and gives a big sigh.

She says, 'It's *tough* being the odd one out.'

I'm hoping Grandma will say something to make me feel better.

Grandma thinks some more and says, '*Very tough.*'

That's not helping, Grandma...

I say, 'Juna's with Elsie, so I said I had to come home for a guitar lesson.'

Grandma looks surprised because it's not true. There are certain rules to not telling the truth. I've said it before, but it is important: polite lies - when you don't want to hurt someone's feelings are usually OK. Gramps will say, 'Dinner is lovely, dear. The burnt bits give it flavour.' But telling lies just because you feel like it, is *very dodgy*, and no one in their right mind would introduce themselves by saying: *Hello everyone. I'm a really good liar.*

Grandma winks at me and says, 'Get your guitar.'

She makes herself a cup of coffee and settles down in her armchair. I play the E, A and D song and I have a go at singing it as well. Grandma joins in, and Herman trots into the kitchen and pins his ears back to listen. Then Eliza pads in, jumps on Grandma's knee and hides her head in Grandma's cardigan. It seems to be going well until Eddie sticks his head round the door and yells, 'Put a sock in it, will you? It's *torture!*'

Grandma cries, '**EDDIE!**'

That seems to be the final straw for me. I run to my bedroom. I am just about to slam the door and, WHAM, a thought hits me between the eyes: *The reason that Elsie got chosen to be in the play is because she has a lovely singing voice. And the reason I didn't, is because I don't.* I have no talent. *At all.* I'm rubbish.

I'm about to burst into tears again when the doorbell rings. I see Elsie out of the window.

Grandma lets her in. I want the ground to swallow me up, but the floor is pretty solid.

I hear Grandma come up the stairs. She comes in, sits down, and takes my hand.

'This is an important lesson, Ellie,' she says. 'We all find out that we're good at some things and not so good at others.'

'I stink,' I say.

Grandma does not contradict me. I feel angry and upset - and I'm also scared that Elsie and I won't be best friends any more – and all because of this STUPID PLAY!

She says, 'You're upset -'

'How did you guess?' I say crossly and immediately regret it.

Grandma doesn't react. 'It's how you handle yourself that counts. Can I give you some advice?'

I nod, because Grandma is full of advice, and most of it is pretty helpful, like: *how to deal with embarrassment* (just get *over* it); and *how to do things you really don't want to do* (just get *on* with it).

'Your special gift,' she says, 'is thinking outside the box. Not everyone can do that. You ask questions that other people don't think to ask.'

I'm surprised. I say, 'If a question is thought but not asked, doesn't it count as a question?'

Grandma smiles. 'That's what I'm talking about,' she says. 'Life is a bumpy road, Ellie, and it won't always lead you to where you want to go. Sometimes you just need to go with the flow, and this is one of those times. You're not in the play, but that frees you up to do something else. Imagine a stream tumbling down a hillside to a river flowing with good ideas and happy thoughts. Jump in and be carried along. Water can't run uphill now, can it?'

Mum and Fin are home from preschool. We go downstairs and find them all in the kitchen.

Mum says 'Elsie's been telling me she's in the play.'

I guess Elsie has also told Mum that I'm *not* in the play because Mum looks pretty anxious. But I don't want her to feel that way. She has enough on her plate. I imagine the stream tumbling towards the River of Good Ideas and Happy Thoughts. I jump in. Grandma's right. Water *can't* run uphill.

I say, 'You will be a big hit, Elsie. You've got a lovely voice.'

Elsie is very pale. She says, 'I can't do it. It's too scary and so is Abigail.'

'Miss Askew is an expert and she chose you because you're the best,' I say. 'Abigail Jennings can take a running jump. What was Miss Askew *thinking?*'

Mum gives me a warning look. She says, 'It's just a confidence issue, Elsie.'

'The more you do something,' says Grandma, 'the less afraid you'll be. You just need practice. Let's sing together now.'

'Good idea,' says Mum. 'What shall we sing?'

I say, 'Over The Rainbow,' because Elsie and I know that song off by heart. Then I think: *Oh no, I can't sing for toffee!*

Fin goes to get his toy microphone.

Mum says, 'After three. One, two, three.'

I sing very quietly and concentrate on listening - and it's plain that Elsie has the sweetest voice. Grandma's voice has a funny wobble and is a bit scratchy, and Mum seems to chase the right notes, but she doesn't always catch them.

Fin sings, 'Over the rainbow, over the rainbow, over the rainbow.'

Elsie closes her eyes. Mum signals to the rest of us to shush. We stop singing, but Elsie carries on – and it's lovely.

When Elsie finishes the song and opens her eyes, we all give her a big clap and Eddie puts his head round the door and says, 'Oh, it's you singing, Elsie. I thought it was Ellie.'

I know Eddie is trying to suck up by telling a BIG FAT LIE, and I suppose I'll have to live with that.

It's a stormy night. I lie in bed trying to sleep. I'm tired and my thoughts are a jumbled mess. I imagine standing by a stream, but the water is dark and cold and there are lots of rocks beneath the surface. I don't even want to dip my toe... How do I know where the stream will carry me?

I hear Herman sniffing. He always seems to know when I can't sleep. I get up and let him in. I curl up on the window seat under my knitted blanket. I'm not brooding on the fact that I can't sing for toffee. Not much anyway. Before too long, Herman settles down and starts to snore and I start to feel sleepy. I'm just about to get into bed when I notice a red light below the rotating beam of the lighthouse. It goes off, then it comes on in the shape of the letter 'I'. And then it disappears.

Don't be alone with a lone, loan shark

This is the **WORST NEWS EVER!** I can't tell you how bad it is. And now, I am truly *glad* and *relieved* that I have *not* been chosen to be in the play. Honestly! Wait for it… the leading boy is… GILBY FLYNN. Yuck, yuck, *SUPER YUCK!*

And guess what – Gilby Flynn's character is really **HORRIBLE.** *Quelle surprise!* (French for *what a shocker… NOT!*)

Let me tell you a little bit about Gilby. He's a BULLY. He calls people names. He pushes people around – especially younger kids. Oh, and he's a bit of a vandal. Gilby Flynn is a *menace.*

We sit round the kitchen table having our dinner and everyone wants to know all about the play. So, I start to explain.

The play is about a really mean man called Charlie (played by Gilby) who is ROTTEN to the core. Everyone can see it, except his *l-o-n-g* suffering girlfriend, Clara, who just wants to get married and have a happy life. But Charlie is *way too busy* making a fortune by lending money to poor people and making them pay back heaps of cash.

I say, 'And if they can't pay it back he says he's going to *hurt* them, so everyone is terrified of him and they have to give up their kids because they can't afford to feed them.'

Gramps says, 'There's a bloke you wouldn't want to meet on a dark night.'

I say, 'And silly Clara doesn't realise he's A PIG.'

'Love is blind,' says Nanna.

She seems to give Dad a dirty look.

Eddie says, 'Pigs are nice, intelligent animals, Ellie.'

I say, 'Oh well, he's a SLIMY SNAKE then.'

'Another misconception,' says Eddie. 'People think snakes are slimy, but they're not.'

'He's a LOAN shark,'* says Gramps.

I say, '*Thank you,* Gramps. You're right. He's a nasty, *lone* shark and Clara ends up looking after these poor, abandoned kids and doing tons of housework.'

Nanna says, 'Sounds like she's got a raw deal,' and for some reason, she looks at Mum.

I say, 'That's right, Nanna. She doesn't realise he's being so unfair and when she asks him to help her out, he says: *Are you nuts? I've got more important things to do.*' Mum looks at Dad who seems fascinated with his green beans. 'Charlie storms off and Clara wanders around in a daze. Then she picks up a photograph of Charlie and sings goodbye to the man she thought she knew. It's really yucky.'

Dad swallows a bean the wrong way and starts to choke. Nanna gives his back a mighty thump. I had no idea she was that strong.

I wait for him to stop coughing, then I say, 'Clara needs to feed the kids though, so she disguises herself and asks Charlie for a heap of cash, even though she will *never* be able to pay it back.'

'Oh, she'll pay it back all right,' says Nanna bitterly. 'She'll cook his meals and wash his underpants.'

Dad takes his glasses off and fiddles with them – then he has a sip of water.

Dad says nervously, 'I'd like to remind everyone that I cooked dinner last week. And thank you, Flora, for washing my underpants.'

Oh dear. My parents are getting muddled up.

I say, 'This story isn't about you.'

There's an awkward silence. They don't look at one another and they don't look happy.

'Finish the story, Ellie,' says Grandma with a sad smile.

'Well,' I say, 'Clara decides to *stand up* to Charlie because, actually, he's just a mean, selfish bully! And in the end, Charlie realises he *stinks*, and if he doesn't want to end up a sad old giffer -'

'Ellie!' says Dad crossly. 'Where do you get these terrible expressions from?'

'Gramps,' I say.

'Oh,' says Dad and frowns at Gramps, who really couldn't care less.

I say, 'If he doesn't want to end up a sad old... *gentleman*... he has to change.'

'Like knowing how to use the dishwasher,' says Grandma, flashing a meaningful look at Dad.

'I do know how to use the dishwasher!' says Dad. 'I used it recently.'

'If two months ago was recent - then, yes, Walter, you did,' says Mum crisply.

Things are getting very tense. Time to wind this story up.

'So he gives his money to the children and he asks Clara to forgive him. And then they have to kiss. YUCK! *The end*,' I say.

'And what does Elsie think of the plot?' asks Grandma.

'She wonders what she's got herself into,' I say.

And it's funny that, even though this is a brand new play, no one is surprised with the plot, except me! Dad says it's a metaphor for rampant capitalism, and Mum says, rather crossly, it's just bog-standard life. Grandma says that casting Gilby Flynn should come with a red warning light. I would have thought Miss Askew would write about happy children, bluebirds and rainbows. I'm quite shocked, really.

Later, I hear Mum and Dad in the den having *words* again.

Dad mutters something, then he says 'There's no peace. It's hard to be creative in a house full of people.'

'Join the club!' Mum snaps. 'I think writing might be a bit more fun than stuffing a washer with other people's pants.'

I sit on the stairs and listen for a few minutes. When Mum and Dad argue, it makes me feel tired and wrung out inside. Herman doesn't like it either. He frowns and pins his ears back. We go to my bedroom and I close the door. I sit watching the lighthouse for a while, but there's no red light tonight.

There should be. A red light is a warning.

An 'oh' at the end

Elsie's mum, Cadence, is a bit stressed. This is to do with her birthday - she's going to be forty. I don't understand the problem, because my mum is already forty-six, and Dad is going to be fifty on Christmas Eve. Grandma says it's something to do with having an 'oh' at the end – and grown-ups don't like that. I didn't feel that way when I turned ten and I won't feel upset when I turn twenty, either. Maybe it starts happening when you're thirty?

Here's a list of things that are wrong at the moment

1. Nanna and Gramps are a bit fed up with us - and we're definitely a bit fed up with them. Dad wasn't keen on the idea of Nanna and Gramps coming to live with us, and now I understand why. Nanna is pretty bossy. She likes things done in a certain way - like the pots have to be washed up in the sink the minute you've finished eating - so there's no chance to sit and chat, and she will not use the dishwasher. She says it's NEW FANGLED and COMPLICATED, but all you have to do is put the pots in and press a button.

2. Nanna is getting on Grandma's nerves because, after all, this is Grandma's house and she's very proud of her new dishwasher. Grandma seems a bit flat. Her body is nice and plump but, inside, there must be a big weight that's pressing on the bit where happiness is stored. I think it's in your head somewhere and maybe your heart.

3. Dad is so involved with his book about the Watford Warbler, that he's in his office ALL the time and he's not helping around the house. This is getting on Mum's nerves because she wants to do more than pick up pants and listen to opera music belting out all day, which Dad plays to give him inspiration. I keep my room tidy but Eddie is messy and Fin is too small to tidy his own room.

4. Cadence is acting funny lately, but not funny, ha ha. She frowns and she sometimes closes the cupboard doors in the café with a BANG. She definitely doesn't want to be forty.

5. Elsie is ÜBER-STRESSED (as Susannah would say) about the school play and, to be honest, I don't blame her. Wild horses wouldn't make me kiss Gilby Flynn, though Miss Askew says it's just a little hug and a peck on the cheek. But still, YUCK!

6. Oh, and then there's Cooper Platt. Something's not quite right with Cooper and I'm worried about him. He's in the same class as Gilby and they

like the same girl, Abigail Jennings, which makes
Gilby and Cooper arch-enemies. I don't know why
Cooper likes Abigail. She never smiles. Cooper
sort of became our friend when he helped us
decorate the Box Brownie café in the summer.

That's six worries, which is half a dozen, and I could box them up like a carton of eggs. And here's another – I think Juna Budd is *trouble*. And one more - the red warning light from the lighthouse. What's *that* all about?

The good news is: Miss Askew has given me a job as her assistant because, she says, I am *organised* and *methodical*, and I think that has something to do with the fact that I make a lot of lists. It means that I can give Elsie support - and I can also keep my eye on Gilby, Abigail and Juna. I have to make sure that all the actors and understudies have a copy of the script and know what time to turn up for rehearsals.

After school, when we've done our homework, Elsie and I go to my bedroom to rehearse. Grandma and Herman come with us to help Elsie get used to performing because she's still very nervous. Grandma settles herself on the window seat and Herman lies on the rug. I play Charlie.

CLARA: Charlie dear, can we start planning our wedding?

CHARLIE: That's your department, Clara. My job is to turn up on the day.

[I try to sound like Gilby, which makes us giggle. Grandma says to Herman, 'He's not very romantic, is he?'

Herman wags his tail.]

CLARA: Our wedding will be so beautiful.

CHARLIE: Make it as beautiful as you want - just stick to the budget.

CLARA: But £50 doesn't go very far, Charlie.

[Grandma says, 'He's tight, as well.']

CHARLIE: Stop nagging, Clara. Money doesn't grow on trees.

[I say, 'Well, there's a shocker.' Then I say, 'That's not in the script, Grandma - that's me.']

CLARA: I'm sorry Charlie. Forgive me.

[I say, 'What's she sorry for? Is she nuts?' Elsie giggles.]

CLARA: You work so hard. Can't you take a day off?

CHARLIE: Time is money, Clara. I can't afford to spend it with you.

CLARA: There's a saying, my dear, that there's more to life than money.

CHARLIE: Like what?

CLARA SINGS:

We have to work, we have to toil and with my hands I dig the soil.
I plant my dreams and hope they sprout,
to show me what life's all about.
I cannot plant a money tree but without love, where would we be?
Charlie dear, please tell me now, if you will make your wedding vow -
to hold me close when life is sad, and dance with me when we are glad -

and love me always, every day. I'll love you always, come what may.

CHARLIE: Love, love, love! Anyone would think love is all you need.

CHARLIE SINGS: [I attempt to sing - it's not good.]

Being wed is like making a bed – I have to have somewhere to lie -

and everyone knows through life's highs and life's lows, your job is to straighten my tie.

My life is outside, in the world broad and wide, lending money to those who aren't rich.

I charge a fat fee, I break the odd knee and sort out the occasional glitch.

It's a jungle out there and I need you to care about ironing my shirts and straightening my chair - cleaning my house and cooking my food, and making quite sure you're in the right mood - at the end of the day, when I come home to roost, in need of your lurve and a giant ego boost.

'I hope Miss Askew addresses these awful gender issues in the text,' says Grandma.

'Oh, she does. Charlie has to take responsibility for his behaviour and recognise that women are equal partners,' I say. 'By the way, Grandma, what's a *giant ego boost*?'

Grandma ponders then says, 'It's like being chosen to write a book about an up-and-coming opera singer.'

Oh. This makes me think: *Dad's not like Charlie, is he?* But Dad would *never* break anyone's knee – not on purpose anyway, though since he started writing the book about the opera singer, he's been, what is commonly known as, *a pain in the butt,* and Mum's right – he hasn't used the dishwasher lately.

It's windy. My bedroom window is creaking, so I get out of bed to ask Dad if he will close it tight-shut. I go downstairs and hear Mum and Dad having words *again.* Flappy ears run in our family, so when you hear someone talking (not very quietly) on the other side of a closed door, you more or less have to listen. It's like a scene from a TV soap.

Mum: I'm sick of hearing about your book, Walter. Get off your high horse.

Dad: (Trying to sound calm) A common idiom,* Flora - but at the moment, I couldn't sit astride a Shetland pony.

Mum: Why do you always do this?

Dad: Do what, Flora?

Mum: Correct me. You're infuriating. You're pompous and self-important. Let me tell you something, Walter: you spend all day thinking about what you should write, when you should be thinking about what you should say.

Dad: To whom, Flora?

Mum: To ME, Walter. YOUR WIFE!

Dad mumbles something, then Mum says, 'What's the point of having a husband if he's always holed up in his ivory tower?' Her voice sounds a bit broken and then, I think, she starts to cry.

Oh. I didn't expect that. I creep back to my bedroom. Listening to the wind howl isn't half as scary as hearing my parents argue. If this were a soap, I would switch it off and never watch it again.

A bit about SELF IMPORTANCE

1. **SELF IMPORTANCE** is thinking that you are a bit special and making sure everybody knows it.
2. **SELF IMPORTANCE** gets on people's nerves.
3. **SELF IMPORTANCE** is not the same as being IMPORTANT.

Our cove is very rocky. The lighthouse sweeps its white light to warn ships to keep a safe distance. Here on dry land, it's rocky too. There's DANGER in the air. It's not a good feeling.

L-I-E is not the truth

It's a stressful day at school. I lose my bag, I'm late for gym and I'm getting a sore throat. Rehearsal doesn't go well. Some people don't turn up and most forget their lines. In the scene when Charlie realises he's as nice as a worm pie – he has to sing the *'I'm sorry, please forgive me'* song to Elsie. Miss Askew tells Gilby to look deeply into Elsie's eyes and tenderly touch her face before he hugs and kisses her. From the side of the stage I see Gilby reach out and pinch Elsie's ear really hard. Elsie flinches and stumbles back - but Miss Askew doesn't see it.

She says, 'Well done, Gilby. That was intense. Let's have more of that, please.'

Gilby smirks, 'Sure, Miss Askew. I'll try.'

Elsie is too shocked to say *anything*.

On the way home, Elsie begs me not to mention it at home, because she's pretty sure that *my* mum will tell *her* mum, and she doesn't want *her* mum to get stressed.

Winter has arrived. It's a windy-rainy night, and it's *so* cold! There's a chill-factor, which means the air feels like it's frozen. That's because the wind is coming from Russia, where there's tons of snow and ice. A white Christmas is predicted – which is quite a nice thought – but I wish there was such a thing as warm snow.

I don't want to be around my family tonight. Fin, my little brother, has a cold and he's snotty and miserable. Grandma seems sad and lonely – even though she has a houseful of people living with her. And Mum doesn't like Dad.

I curl up on my window seat with a book, a glass of chocolate milk and a Tupperware dish of mandarin oranges. I'm reading about a girl detective called Roxy who stumbles on all sorts of mysteries and solves them fearlessly. I hear Herman sniffing at the door, so I let him in. He puts his head in my lap and I tickle his ears. I've not seen the red light or any red glowing letters for a couple of nights now.

Then, just below the circling white beam of the lighthouse, there's a red flash. And then, the letter 'E', glows in the dark.

STRANGE! What would Roxy do, I wonder?

She would be *methodical* and she would *think* and she would *problem solve.*

I grab my notepad and a pen. I write down the time: 8:57, and the letters I have seen so far: L – I – E.

Well, LIE is a word, but it has two meanings. When I say *lie* to Herman, he flops down and has a snooze. When I say *don't lie* to Fin, it means - stop trying to get me into trouble, you little weasel.

I go down to the kitchen to see if there's someone friendly to chat to – but there's no one. Dad will be in his office – or as Mum now calls it – his *ivory tower*. Grandma will be in her sitting room listening to jazz or reading a book. Nanna and Gramps go to bed early with a whisky and water, and Mum has left a message on the kitchen table: *Gone to have a drink with Cadence. Don't wait up.* And when was it *ever* a good idea to chat to Eddie?

I don't feel well and I'm lonely. I look at Herman who looks a bit worried but wags his tail anyway. He seems to know I need a human to talk to. And then I think of Jack. He's a bit older and he's creative and clever. He might be able to help. Eddie's laptop is open on the kitchen table. I sit down and type an email.

TO: Jack Bell
SUBJECT: URGENT! Please read!

Hi Jack,
C'est moi, Ellie. Sometimes at night a red light flashes on and off at the lighthouse – and then a red letter appears. These are the letters I've seen so far: L and I. Tonight it was E. I don't know what the letters mean.

Gilby Flynn pinched Elsie's ear in rehearsal. He hurt her. Elsie won't tell her mum and she won't let me tell mine. Gilby is a BULLY. I do NOT like him and I NEVER WILL.

PS Do you think the red letters are a coded message?

I hear Eddie whistling a tune that Susannah plays on her

guitar, so I click SEND and jump off the stool. Eddie comes into the kitchen looking like he's been fighting a storm. His coat is wet.

'Where have you been?' I ask.

Eddie ignores my question.

He says, 'I've just put my car keys down and now I can't find them. I was supposed to be at Susannah's an hour ago.'

I see his keys on the dresser. Normally I would give him a good telling off. Susannah's going to dump him again if he doesn't shape up.

Instead, I hand him his keys and say, 'You go, Eddie. I'll log off for you.'

'Are you ill?' asks Eddie sarcastically and dashes off.

Jack has his own laptop, so I'm hoping he will check his email and write straight back.

While I'm waiting, I Google: LIE. I follow a link:

A lie is not the truth. It is a false statement made with the intention to deceive.

And then, a message from Jack pops into the inbox.

FROM: Jack Bell
TO: Menella Booton
SUBJECT: RE: URGENT! Please read!

Hi Ellie,
First. This is VERY SERIOUS. You must tell your Mum about Gilby. Tell her NOW!

Second: I've never seen a red light flashed from the lighthouse before. That's interesting. No idea what the letters mean. Let me know if you see any more.
Jack
PS Is the red light static, or does it go round?

Jack's email actually *invites* a response from me. I feel better already.

I reply:

OK. Thanks for the advice. The red light is static. I'll let you know if I see any more letters.

I shut down Eddie's laptop. Herman is asleep in his basket. I pad across the hall. I hear Gramps' and Nanna's snores coming from their bedroom. I climb the stairs and put my ear to Dad's door. He's on the telephone and he doesn't like to be disturbed. I can hear jazz music playing softly from Grandma's sitting room. She's dozing with a book on her lap. I even put my head into Fin's room. He's all scrunched up with his bottom in the air.

I feel all alone.

S is for SPOOKY

Saturday: I wake up in the early hours to check the lighthouse, but there is no sign of red lights or red letters. I go back to bed and toss and turn.

It feels like I've only been asleep two minutes when Mum yells up the stairs, 'Ellie? I'm going to the Box Brownie for coffee. Do you want to come?'

I yell back, 'Please. Wait for me.'

I run to the bathroom, flick a flannel across my face, wash my hands and brush my teeth. I pull on jeans and a woolly jumper and hurry downstairs. Mum's hair is messy. She looks tired and a bit scruffy.

She sits Fin on the stairs and helps him put on wellies.

She says, 'Have you had breakfast?'

If I say no, will she make me stay behind?

She eyes me suspiciously then says, 'You can have scrambled eggs and a glass of milk.'

I'd rather have waffles and a milkshake, but I don't argue. I take Fin's hand, and we walk down the hill to the Box Brownie.

'Mum…' I say.

But Fin starts talking about what *he* wants for breakfast, even though he's already had a boiled egg and bread soldiers, and I can't get a word in edgeways.

Elsie is there helping Cadence. She waves at me when I go in, and I notice she's got her hair in a pony tail, but it's not her usual style – it's loose over her ears. I sit at the counter on a tall stool.

I say, 'What's with the hairdo?'

Elsie pulls her hair back from her right ear. I see an awful blue and purple bruise. I gasp. She quickly covers it up and gives me a little smile, but it's not what you would call a happy smile.

'Elsie, you've got to tell your mum,' I hiss.

Elsie butters bread and ignores me. I feel sick inside. This is a terrible secret.

I look around. Mum sits at the far end of the counter, talking to Cadence. There are people munching quietly, gazing out to sea. Others read newspapers and sip coffee. Some chat. The coffee machine hisses and glugs. Everything seems so normal. Then I notice Juna Budd squeezed into a corner. I've never seen her at the Box Brownie before. She's on her own, of course, doodling on a bit of paper. I wonder if she will sense me and look up? She doesn't. I wonder if Elsie asked her to come?

I move to sit closer to Mum. Cadence rubs her head.

I hear her say: 'One glass of wine too many. Never again.'

Mum says, 'Well I don't regret it. We needed to get things off our chests.'

And together they both say, '*Men!*'

Cadence is very pretty. She has red bouncy hair like

Elsie. Today it's pinned up and shows her long, pale neck. She wears high heels, swishy frocks and red lipstick and she likes to dance. She's divorced from Elsie's dad, who Elsie doesn't see at all.

In the summer, Eddie told me that Jem, a *Greengrocer, Fruitier & Purveyor of Fine Foods* - has a 'thing' for Cadence. This means that he really, *really* likes her. I'm expecting Jem to marry Cadence sometime soon.

Cadence says, 'Well, if Jem is more interested in Maggie Bell, then good luck to him. You can't count on *any* man, *and that's the truth.*'

My ears start to flap. Maggie Bell is Jack's auntie, and she's a teacher at our school.

Mum says, 'Don't jump to conclusions, Cadence. Jem's a good man. You need to talk to him.' She sips her coffee then shakes her head sadly. 'But talking to Walter is a waste of time. There's no point any more.'

Mum notices me, smiles weakly and stops talking. You know, of course, that Walter is my dad. But Cadence hasn't noticed me.

She says, 'Marriage is a very small boat on a very big sea, Flora. If you stop communicating you hit the rocks, *and that's the truth.*'

Hitting the rocks sounds serious. I have a communication problem too. I need to tell Mum about Gilby bruising Elsie's ear, and I probably should tell her about the red letters flashed from the lighthouse.

Suddenly, I think: *RED! WARNING! L-I-E! Does that mean DON'T tell a lie, or DO tell a lie?*

41

Mum looks at me strangely.

She says, 'Are you all right, Ellie?'

Then I see Elsie's look of panic and for some reason I say, 'Sure,' in a casual way that shocks me.

I concentrate on my scrambled eggs the way Gramps concentrates on his potatoes.

I walk home with Mum and Fin, leaving Elsie helping Cadence and Juna hiding in her corner. I don't feel good about Juna. There's something about her that's just not right. Mum's not talkative and when we get home she gets her shopping bag, straps Fin in his car seat, and drives off. She doesn't even ask if I'd like to go with them. I put my head round the workshop door and see Eddie working at his bench, which is strange because he usually has weekends off.

'Not now, Melly Moo,' he says. 'Very busy.' When I don't move he says rudely, 'Push off!'

It's good to have a dog like Herman who is always glad to see me. I get his lead out of the captain's chest in the hall. He comes thundering down the stairs, wagging his tail so much I think he might fall over. Dad's in his office. I know he is, because I hear him shout, 'Crazy dog!' and then slam the door.

I go to the whiteboard in the kitchen and I write:

Time: 10:23 Gone to the beach with Herman

I resist the temptation to add: *Not that anybody cares.*

Grandma says dogs can talk. I don't know about that, but I do know that dogs have thoughts and feelings, and if anyone thinks they don't – they're most certainly, almost definitely wrong. When we reach the slipway to the beach, I let Herman off his lead. He doesn't run off like he normally does. He sits down and looks at me with a worried expression.

I hug him and say, 'I'm all right, Herman. I'm worried and a bit lonely, that's all.'

I tell him what's on my mind. He listens, even though he wants to run into the sea and have a splash, which is one of his most favourite things to do.

I say, 'Gilby is a rotten bully, and I've seen red letters flashed from the lighthouse - and Juna Budd is hanging around Elsie. She doesn't like me and I don't like her. And nobody is happy – not even Grandma. And I've no idea what LIE means.'

Herman wags his tail and lies down. I laugh. He is a super-smart dog.

I get his ball out of my pocket and throw it as far as I can. He chases it and brings it back and then he runs into the sea for a splash.

I'm walking and thinking and sometimes talking to Herman. Before I know it, we're at the end of the cove. It's a rocky climb up to the lighthouse from the beach, but it's fine so long as the tide is out and you're wearing sensible shoes. Herman bounds over the rocks and shows me the easiest way to climb up.

I grab hold of tufty grass and pull myself to the top. And there, the lighthouse is in full view like a giant white chess piece. There's nobody about. A seagull sits on the gate.

Herman bounds up to say hello and it flies off with a screech. I push the gate open and walk up to the lighthouse.

There are steps up to the door. I walk past them, circle round and get to the point where I can see the Box Brownie café on the promenade and my house on the hill above it. I look at the lighthouse. About twenty metres up, there's a narrow window. I've never really noticed it before. This must be where the red light shines from.

The wind starts to pick up. There are dark clouds and the light suddenly dims. I shiver and make my way out of the garden. Herman is keen to go as well. Just as I get to the gate, I see something caught on the latch. It's a small piece of red and yellow checked fabric.

We climb down and run along the sand. I like to sing on an empty beach when the waves are crashing down - but now I know that I can't sing for toffee, so I don't even try.

Climbing up the slipway, I see a figure going past. It's Juna Budd. She doesn't notice me. Her hands are in her pockets and her head is down.

When I reach home, I sit on the old bench in the garden and look down at the beach. I think about Juna and why I don't like her. When I see her, I feel funny inside – but not funny, ha ha. I think it's because she doesn't talk much, or smile, or show any interest in answering questions. She ignores people and wanders around by herself. When you wander around with no place to go, does that mean you're lost?

It's night. Nanna and Gramps are snoring. It's the only

thing they do together without bickering. Dad is blasting opera music from his ivory tower. Eddie is out. Mum has gone to bed early and Grandma is reading in her sitting room. I sit on my window seat. The beam from the lighthouse sweeps into my bedroom and sweeps out again. Herman is sniffing for his ball under the bottom bunk. I switch on my light and have a look. I'm an organised person. There are plastic boxes of felt-tips and crayons, paper, and card – a box for scissors, glue, staples and string. There's a box of plastic paper that Grandma gave me. You can write on it, crumple it up, soak it in water, and it stays as good as new! Someday I'll find a use for it. I see Herman's ball and reach for it. He chews it for a while then flops down and goes to sleep. I switch off my light and sit in the dark. I start to nod off.

And then…

The red light! It's on. It goes off. Then it comes back on in the shape of an S. It stays on for a minute, then disappears, and there's just the white beam of the lighthouse sweeping round and round.

Add the S to L-I-E, and you get LIES! I *don't* tell lies. But I'm not telling the truth either. This is getting very spooky.

R U OK and M for mess

Sometimes Grandma goes to church. Not every Sunday – only when she feels like it.

She says, 'You don't have to go to church to be close to God, but sometimes, the only place to find a bit of peace is in God's house.'

I wonder why Grandma needs to find peace? I almost ask what's bothering her – but I don't, because I have enough troubles of my own.

Eddie chomps his way through breakfast, slurps his tea and checks his email, then says he's got things to do in the workshop. Eddie would *never* work on a Sunday unless something was really urgent. I ask him if I can check my emails. He grunts, and I choose to interpret this as *yes*.

There's an email from Jack, who normally writes when there's a blue moon.

FROM: Jack Bell
TO: Menella Booton
SUBJECT: R U OK?

Hi Ellie,
What did your mum say? Are you and Elsie OK?

Any more red letters? I was thinking – you might have missed some letters, or there might be more to come. It might be a code. Funny coincidence – L,I,E are all the letters needed to spell your name! Keep me informed. Jack

PS. I wonder who the message is for, and who is sending it?

I think: *Oh no! Jack thinks I've told Mum about Gilby! I have* to speak to Elsie! I grab my coat and pop my head round the kitchen door. Fin is on the floor playing with his Moshi Monsters. Mum sits at the table looking at her hands.

I say, 'I'm going to see Elsie.'

Mum says, 'OK.'

She doesn't ask me when I'll be back, or tell me to fasten my coat.

I say, 'Are you all right, Mum?'

'Sure, Ellie,' she says and smiles, but it's not a happy smile.

'Why don't you have a cup of tea?' I say, because everyone knows that tea makes grown-ups feel better.

Elsie sits at a window table. She sees me and waves. When I get to the café, she's already outside. She grabs my hand and pulls me in the direction of the slipway and we run onto the beach. It's deserted.

I say, 'We've got to do something about Gilby.'

Elsie frowns and lets go of my hand. 'You've not told your mum, have you?' she says.

'No,' I say nervously, 'but I emailed Jack.'

Elsie looks angry and walks away.

'Jack says it's serious,' I call after her. 'Gilby shouldn't be hurting you. We need to tell someone about it.' Elsie keeps walking – hands in pockets, head bowed. She looks lost, like Juna Budd. 'You shouldn't hide it, Elsie.'

'I'm not hiding it,' she says crossly – then she bursts into tears. I hug her. 'What if Mum thinks we should move again?' she sobs.

I know what that's all about. The last time Cadence was stressed, she planned to sell the café and move far away. I understand why Elsie is so scared. This is her home – she doesn't want to leave it.

I say, 'Things have a habit of working out,' because that's what Grandma says, and Grandma is nearly always right. I think that it might be a good idea to change the subject for a while. 'There's something strange going on at the lighthouse,' I say. Then I think: *Why haven't I told Elsie about the red letters before?* I realise I've not been sharing things with Elsie lately. We've sort of grown apart.

I tell her about the red light flashed from the lighthouse and the letters I've seen.

'I'll show you,' I say, and we run to the edge of the cove, clamber over the rocks and pull ourselves onto the grassy bank.

The gate creaks when I push it open. We circle the lighthouse until we're in line with the café and my house on the hill. There are no other buildings in this line of sight and I'm starting to realise the message must be for someone who can see it. The café is closed at night, the promenade is deserted, but my home is always full of people, day and night.

I point to the window. 'That's where the light is flashed from. Jack said that L-I-E are the letters in my name.'

'But you've seen L-I-E-S, and those are the letters in *my* name,' says Elsie.

We look at one another. This is getting too weird.

'It's Gilby,' she says. 'He's letting us know that if we tell anyone, he will just say we're lying. No one will believe us.'

My heart starts to hammer. It's lonely up here. I feel a drop of rain. A gust of wind blows Elsie's hair from her face and I see her bruised ear. My tummy flips and I shiver.

We make our way back to the gate. Elsie stops and frowns. She picks up the scrap of checked fabric, caught on the latch.

'I'm sure I've seen this before,' she says.

She puts the scrap in her pocket.

The tide is coming in and the waves swallow up the beach. We pick our way along the edge of the cornfield, and climb over the fence to get back onto the promenade. The Box Brownie café twinkles in the distance. It's raining hard now, so we start to run. I just want to get inside - feel warm, feel safe.

As we pass a shelter, someone jumps out. It's Gilby Flynn.

He blocks our way and says, 'Running in your smelly boots, smelly girl?'

There are others inside the shelter. My mouth is suddenly

dry.

I swallow hard and say, 'Trainers, actually,' because Dad says even when you can't *stand* someone, you can still be polite. I look at his feet. He steps towards me.

'Look!' I say. 'We're wearing the same brand.'

His minions laugh – a bit at me, a bit at him. These boys aren't pin ups: they're tall, with greasy hair and spots. I notice Abigail Jennings, the policeman's daughter, puffing on a cigarette. Gilby switches his attention to Elsie.

'Want a ciggie, Cranberry?' he says. That's what he calls Elsie because her surname is Berry and she has red hair. He's not very inventive. He reaches out and flicks her hair, exposing her bruised ear. Elsie flinches. Then he says in a stupid baby voice, 'A ciggie might take your mind off your little piggy ear.'

His minions and Abigail go, 'Aww,' and laugh.

Elsie says nothing. She's frozen to the spot.

'Don't want to get lung cancer, thanks,' I say. 'Interesting fact: cranberries are full of vitamin C - good for clearing up spots.'

I stare at his skin and I can feel his anger. Bullies don't like to be told anything. They think they know it all. My legs shake. I grab Elsie's hand and we make a run for it. We burst into the café.

Cadence says, 'Was that the Flynn boy you were talking to? He didn't bother you did he?'

Before I can say anything, Elsie flashes me a look and says, 'No, Mum.'

When I'm sure Gilby and his evil tribe have gone, I go

home. I'm shaking the rain off my coat when Eddie comes out of the den and says, 'You've got another email from Jack. He must be sweet on you.'

I say crossly, 'SHUT YOUR MOUTH, you big ape!'

Whenever I say things like this, (*always* provoked, I might add) Mum somehow overhears.

She appears out of nowhere and says, 'Don't speak to your brother like that.'

This makes me feel even crosser, because Mum doesn't realise that the *last* thing I need is Eddie making *stupid* remarks. Not to mention the fact that my parents aren't exactly speaking to one another politely any more. What's the word? Irony?

Dad, who hears *everything*, appears at the top of the stairs and says, 'The lady doth protest too much.'*

He's said this before. It's a line from a Shakespeare play and it means that if you're too keen to deny something, the opposite *must* be true. So, he thinks that Jack *is* sweet on me, which is so IRRITATING! They have *no idea* what's really going on in my life.

Eddie just laughs. He says, 'The laptop's in the den.'

I stomp up the stairs. I shout, 'I'M BUSY!'

Eddie goes out. Dad goes back to his ivory tower and Mum goes into the kitchen. I stand at the top of the stairs for a minute, then sneak back down and go into the den.

I open the email from Jack.

FROM: Jack Bell
TO: Menella Booton
SUBJECT: Hi

Hi Ellie,
Just checking that everything is OK.
Jack

All that fuss for a few words! I pop my head outside the den. No one is around. I go back and hit the reply button.

Hi Jack,

C'est moi, Ellie. I've seen another red letter from the lighthouse – an S. So now I've seen L,I,E,S. The red light shines from a window. Elsie and I checked out the lighthouse earlier. On the way back we saw Gilby. He was horrible, as usual. Elsie still doesn't want to tell anybody. She's got a big bruise but she's hiding it.

PS. I think the message might be for me, but L-I-E-S are the letters you need to spell Elsie. What do you think is going on?

I send the email to Jack and start to feel nervous and guilty. I know that I'm telling Jack things that I should tell Mum and Dad. I'm not telling my parents the truth. Is that the same as telling them *lies*, as in L,I,E,S? I really don't like this.

I'm just about to shut down Eddie's laptop when there's a

ding. Jack's sent a reply.

Stop messing about. This is SERIOUS, Ellie. We have a zero tolerance policy towards bullying at my school. If someone got hurt, the bully would be excluded. TELL SOMEONE! Jack

I feel sick. I *know* this is SERIOUS! I run upstairs to my bedroom and shut the door.

A list of my worries

1. Gilby has hurt Elsie.
2. Elsie doesn't want to tell her mum about Gilby.
3. Gilby is a main character in the play and Gilby's understudy is Cody Child, who is scared of Gilby. Cody has started to miss rehearsals.
4. So, if Gilby gets excluded (and will that make him bully Elsie even more?) then poor Miss Askew's play will be in BIG TROUBLE, because there'll be no one to play Charlie, which will mean that –
5. Miss Askew will leave the school with bad memories, and things could get even worse for Elsie.

I look at my list.
It's Gilby, Gilby, Gilby, **GILBY!**
That HORRIBLE BOY!
Elsie is always worried about her mum and, although I

don't like admitting it, I worry about mine. Mum seems tired and unhappy. She doesn't like Dad any more – and all Dad seems to do is work, work, WORK. Eddie's a rubbish boyfriend to Susannah again - scruffy and always late. Nanna and Gramps do *nothing* but bicker, and Grandma seems to have run out of advice and smiles. My family is falling apart and so is Elsie. There's only Herman who stays the same. He's always kind and he loves everybody. I can tell you, it's a bit of a shock when you realise you've only got a dog to rely on.

Every Sunday evening Grandma roasts a chicken. Eddie is vegetarian so he has a Quorn fillet, which is a kind of fungus. That might sound yuck, but it looks like meat and tastes good. I look at my plate of food.

I think: *I like chickens when they're alive and clucking,* and suddenly, I feel sad for the chicken on my plate, and I can't eat.

Eddie keeps looking at me, which is irritating.

He says, 'You're quiet, Melly Moo.'

'So is everybody else,' I snap.

I tell Mum I don't feel well and leave the table. Herman follows me, even though he loves to be around roast chicken.

I sit for a long time on my window seat trying to read a book, but I can't concentrate. The tide is out and there's a long stretch of bleak, empty beach. The promenade is deserted.

The outside security light pops on and I see Eddie

heading for his car. I hope he's going to see Susannah. I hope he's tidied himself up. I hope he's not going to mess up again.

There's a knock on my door. It's Grandma. She comes in with a mug of hot chocolate and a blueberry muffin.

She says, 'That's where you are, Herman. I thought you'd be looking after Ellie.'

Herman smiles and wags his tail. Grandma sits down.

I say, 'Did you find peace in church, Grandma?'

Grandma smiles. 'I did, Ellie. There's something about a church that's very settling.'

She scratches Herman's chin and tickles his velvety ears. When Grandma is around, everything seems better somehow. I've never heard Grandma shout or say anything mean. I've seen her sad, especially after Grandpa died - and I've seen her lonely, even in a house full of people. But, no matter what, Grandma always tries to be understanding and positive.

She says, 'Are you missing a bit of peace, my darling?'

Have you ever noticed, if you're feeling sad and worried and someone is really kind, it's hard to stop sadness spilling out of your eyes? I start to cry.

Grandma puts her arm round me. Herman puts his head in my lap and smacks his chops together. He frowns and his eyes go from me to Grandma, like he's watching a tennis match. He looks like Gromit which makes me laugh. So, I'm crying and laughing at the same time. BIZARRE!

Grandma looks across the cove and says, 'I keep seeing red letters flashed from the lighthouse.'

I gulp. '*Really*, Grandma?'

She nods. 'I've written them down.'

'I've seen some too!' I say.

Grandma looks excited. 'What letters have you seen?'

I say, 'L, I, E, and S.'

Grandma says, 'I've seen those letters, and M as well.'

'Is it a secret message?' I ask.

'I have no idea. I was wondering myself.' Grandma gets my notepad and a pencil and jots down: L-I-E-S-M. 'It might be code,' she says. 'It could be an anagram of LIMES.'

'Or SLIME.' I think: *Gilby would definitely use a word like that. Nasty boy, nasty word.*

'Or SMILE,' says Grandma.

'Oh no,' I say, 'it's *definitely* not SMILE.'

Grandma looks at me. I hold my breath and look away - but Grandma, as usual, is clever.

She says, 'Why wouldn't it be *smile*?'

I ABSOLUTELY DO NOT KNOW WHAT TO SAY!

I shrug and I feel bad, because I realise that it's becoming a habit *not* to tell the truth. I'm in a big M for MESS.

'What's wrong, Ellie? Talk to me,' pleads Grandma.

But I just can't.

Grandma hugs me and says, 'Drink your chocolate before it goes cold. I'll let you know if I see any more letters. We'll be code-crackers. It will be our secret.'

MONDAY - 10

I don't like Mondays. I don't like Tuesdays, Wednesdays or Thursdays. The only bit I like about Friday is home time, when the weekend begins.

I do not want to go to school. I think I have a cold, or a sore throat, or a headache - or all three. I just don't feel good.

I tell Mum, but she just looks through me and says, 'See how you go.'

I know how my day will go. It will be rotten. I get my school bag and step outside. The wind helps me slam the door. No one cares how I feel.

When it's windy, I usually feel like something exciting is about to happen, but today I feel like I've been ironed out flat. I am nothing – I am a piece of waste paper, and the wind can whisk me away and I'll never be heard of, or seen again.

Elsie usually goes to the Box Brownie café and waits for me – but she's not there this morning. There's a rehearsal this evening in the school hall, but I have a guitar lesson, so I can't stay behind. There will be no one to help Elsie if Gilby grabs her again. I battle along the promenade, shoulders hunched. A few of the lamp posts have something tied to them – small posters that say:

10
T

What's *that* all about? I start the climb to town on the other side of the cove. Further up the hill, I recognise Elsie's blue coat and red hair. She didn't wait for me. A girl steps out from Curly Lane. It's Juna Budd with her creepy skull and crossbones bag. She quickens her pace and falls into step with Elsie.

Great! My best friend has gone off with freaky Juna Budd. I stop. I'm one heartbeat from turning round and running home.

Someone shouts, '**ELLIE!**'

It's Cooper Platt hurrying up Curly Lane. By the time he reaches me, he's puffing like a steam train.

'That hill's gonna kill me,' he gasps.

I say, 'It's the cigs that'll kill you.'

Cooper smiles at his shoes, which wouldn't win any awards for style or shine. He's not wearing a coat either, and his school jumper has a hole at the elbow.

'Where's Elsie?' asks Cooper.

'She's gone on ahead.'

'Oh, that's good,' he says. 'I thought she might be sick.'

Since Eddie teased me about Jack, I feel self-conscious. I look at Cooper. I thought he'd volunteered to be a stagehand so he could hang around Abigail, but maybe it's Elsie he likes?

We walk together in awkward silence.

A bit about AWKWARD SILENCE

An awkward silence is a break in the conversation that you just can't fill. This might be for a few reasons:

1. One or both of you might be having private thoughts that you just don't want to share.

I'm wondering: *Why is Cooper so worried about Elsie all of a sudden?*

2. You might be completely BORED and can't be bothered to say anything.

Which is quite rude, because there are TONS of things you could say if you wanted to be polite. Dad calls this PHATIC* communication and hairdressers are very good at it. They ask questions like: Did you do anything nice this weekend?

3. Or both of you might want to say something important - but neither of you know where to begin.

There must be other reasons for AWKWARD SILENCE, but I can't think of them right now.

Just to fill up the silence I say, 'I won't be at rehearsal tonight.'

Cooper says, 'OH NO! I can't go either.'

He looks stricken and I feel *totally confused.*

I say, 'What's going on, Cooper?'

But Cooper just shakes his head and says, 'Nothin'.'

At the school gates we go our separate ways. Later, I see him in the corridor and he gives me a desperate sort of look -

but then just passes by. Elsie is quiet and preoccupied with keeping her hair over her bruised ear. I feel sorry, sad, worried and angry - all at the same time. Juna Budd creeps around like a shadow. When the bell rings at the end of the day, I feel wrung out like a dishcloth. The last thing I feel like doing is playing my guitar. I suck at music – so what's the point?

As I walk through the playground, I see Gilby push Juna roughly against the wall. Her head hits the brick, but she doesn't look up and she says nothing. I suddenly feel very sorry for Juna.

Gilby has stupid names for everyone. He calls Juna Budd, *Tuna Blood.*

He shouts at her, 'HEY TUNA! YOU'RE BLEEDING.' Then, in a silly sing-song voice, *'THE SHARKS ARE COMING TO GET YOU.'*

Juna tries to get past, but he blocks her. Then he sees me.

'What's that PUTRID stink?' he shouts. 'Oh, it's UGLY Smelly-Ellie in her STUPID boots.'

I've suddenly had *enough* of Gilby.

Even though I know it's probably, *almost definitely,* NOT a good idea, I shout back, 'I'M NOT SMELLY – BUT YOU'RE ALWAYS GOING TO BE A SLIMY LITTLE SUCKER,' which is the first thing that pops into my head. It's one of Grandma's expressions.

He's so surprised, Juna's able to wriggle past. I don't wait around. I slip out of the school gates and get lost in the crowd.

I get home and run to my bedroom. Herman sniffs at the door, so I let him in. I kneel down and hug him.

You know how you can set dominoes on their edge, so they can crash into one another? Well – that's my life now. I move to this town – *one domino* – I go to school – *another domino* - I make friends with Elsie – *another domino*. Get the picture? But my life's not stable any more. My parents aren't happy. School isn't fun and Elsie is like a stranger. And now I've got on the wrong side of a BIG BULLY.

One little push and my life will come CRASHING DOWN, I just know it.

THEN WHAT WILL HAPPEN?

I lie on my bed and hide my face. I hear the phone ringing and a few minutes later Mum knocks on my door and pops her head round.

She says, 'Susannah's been delayed. She'll bring her guitar another night.'

I say, 'I didn't really feel like it anyway.'

'You're not getting sick, are you?' she asks.

'I might be,' I say.

I wish Mum would come in and sit down. I want her to ask me questions. I need a hug.

She hesitates for a moment then says, 'Well, see how you go.' She closes the door. She's gone.

I feel empty and completely miserable. I go down to the kitchen but Mum's not there. Grandma is at the sink peeling potatoes and there's casserole in the oven. The smell makes me feel sick.

I say, 'I'm not hungry, Grandma. I'll stay in my

bedroom.'

Grandma looks at me strangely. I manage a fake smile.

She frowns and says, 'All right, Ellie.'

I go back to my room. I'm embarrassed and a bit mortified to admit this - but I start to cry. BIG TIME.

The good thing about living in a house blasted with opera music, is that you can cry your eyes out and no one hears.

But that's not so good really.

Later, there's a knock on my door. It's Susannah.

Susannah isn't like Mum or Dad or Grandma. She's a grown-up, but she's also young. She tells me things about her life that she doesn't tell anyone else. I know she almost got a tattoo of a red-eyed bug on her neck because she felt angry, but changed her mind at the last moment and decided to get a butterfly on her wrist instead. I know that when she was eighteen she got drunk, lost her shoes, fell over, and had to have six stitches in her head. And she *loved* those shoes. So now, she doesn't drink so much and when she met Eddie, she became a vegetarian like him.

She says, 'Sorry I'm late. I thought I'd call in to see you anyway.'

She takes one look at me and says, 'What's wrong, sweetie?'

And, it might come as NO surprise at all, but I start to cry *again.* HELP! What's *wrong* with me? I can't get any words out.

Susannah says, 'Let's go for a walk.'

It's dark outside, but it seems like a good idea.

Susannah goes to have a word with Grandma. I get ready and *of course*, Herman thinks he's invited too. Susannah, Herman and I step into the night. The sky is inky and sprinkled with stars.

Starlight takes a *l-o-n-g* time to reach the earth. Every twinkle in the sky is from the past and set off on its journey long before I was born. Before I was me. Before I had any worries.

The tide is coming in, so we walk along the promenade. Herman is happy. He loves to be outside, sniffing the air, even when it's dark and cold. Walking and talking is good for the soul. Fresh, cold air sweeps thoughts out of dark spaces. Already I feel calmer.

Susannah says, 'I'm sorry for letting you down this evening, Ellie. I was called to an emergency meeting.'

This sounds mysterious.

'What about?' I ask.

Susannah puts her arm round me. 'Secret stuff,' she whispers.

Now I *really* want to know.

She says, 'Miss Askew should have a proper send-off because she's taught at the school for such a long time.'

I agree. When Susannah was at school, Miss Askew realised how musical she was and encouraged her to write songs. Susannah is very fond of Miss Askew and even though she is a bit beige, I'm sad she's leaving and she's not even telling people why.

Susannah says, 'The trouble is, she's forbidden a leaving party.'

'Why?' I ask. A party sounds like a good idea to me. A party usually means presents.

Susannah says, 'She doesn't want to get emotional. I think she's afraid she might break down. Some people are like that – they prefer to keep their feelings hidden. All we can say is, *good luck*. She's heading for a very different life. Rwanda* is a *long* way away.'

I say, 'Rwanda?'

Susannah gasps. 'Oh no! That's a secret.'

I've heard of Rwanda. It's in Africa and there are lots of people needing help there.

'Don't worry,' I say. 'I'm good at keeping secrets.'

We walk on a bit, then she says, 'But not all secrets are good, Ellie. You know that don't you?'

I'm not sure what she's getting at.

Susannah says, 'So if you're worried about something, you should tell someone.'

I say, 'But Miss Askew keeps secrets and so do you.'

Susannah nods and thinks. 'I suppose the difference is - they're not *total* secrets. They're shared with trusted people.'

We get to the end of the promenade and turn to walk back. Herman stops to sniff a lamp post with a 10-T poster tied to it.

'What does 10-T mean?' I ask.

She shrugs. 'No idea.'

When we get home, Grandma has baked scones and they're hot out of the oven. Eddie comes out of the workshop sniffing the fruity air. He's always working late now, which isn't like him at all. For some reason, Susannah doesn't seem to mind. Nanna and Gramps are in bed, of course. They don't vary their routine for anyone. If the world was to end at midnight, they would still go to bed at nine o'clock with a glass of whisky and water. Susannah makes hot chocolate and laughs at Eddie who has Superman underpants showing above his jeans. Eddie drops a kiss on her head. Susannah makes Eddie seem human. Well, almost. I couldn't imagine my family without her.

'Where's Mum?' I ask Grandma.

Grandma looks concerned. She says, 'She has a headache so she went to bed.'

There's opera music blasting from Dad's office, so I know where *he* is. If Mum's got a headache, he could turn it down a bit.

I eat a scone and drink hot chocolate. It's nice to sit with Grandma, Susannah and even Eddie.

Susannah's right though. I am keeping secrets.

TUESDAY - 9

Tuesday morning, 8:17am. The Box Brownie café is open, but Elsie isn't there. Cadence sees me and opens the door.

She says, 'Elsie didn't come down to the café this morning, Ellie. She went straight to school.'

I say, 'Oh. OK,' and pull my mouth into the shape of a smile.

'Is everything all right?' asks Cadence, looking worried.

I nod and try to look cheerful.

I say, 'Bye,' and hurry off along the promenade.

There are posters tied to lamp posts, flapping in the wind. I take a closer look. They're tied with green stripy string - but, this morning, they're different. They say:

9
H

I tug one off and stuff it in my pocket. I'm starting to wonder if they're connected with the red letters from the lighthouse.

I see Cooper further up the hill. I shout to him and he waits for me, hands in his pockets, shivering.

'Why don't you wear a coat?' I ask.

'I don't feel the cold,' he says. But he looks pretty cold to me. 'I went to the rehearsal last night,' he mutters.

'You did?'

'I had a doctor's appointment -' he breaks off to cough '- but it wasn't worth going.'

'You should have gone,' I say.

Cooper gives me a strange look - like he's going to say something, but he doesn't.

'Did everyone remember their lines?' I ask.

He smiles. 'Everyone except Gilby. I think I put him off.'

I say, 'Oh.' We walk on and there's another AWKWARD SILENCE. I'm thinking: *What's going on?*

A bit more about AWKWARD SILENCE

1. If a silence is awkward maybe it's just waiting to be filled with SOMETHING.

2. Maybe that SOMETHING might as well be a good, HONEST question.

So I say, 'Do you want to tell me something, Cooper?'

Another awkward silence. Cooper keeps his head down.

I feel TOTALLY frustrated with him. This is so annoying! There's something wrong, I just know it - and he won't tell me.

Then I think: *O-Oh – is this what I'm doing?*

Grandma: Is anything wrong, Ellie?

Me: No, Grandma (LIE)

Mum: Are you all right, Ellie?

Me: Yes, Mum. (LIE)

Susannah: What's wrong, sweetie?

Me: Nothing, Susannah. (LIE)

And I've always thought that I don't lie. I take a deep breath. I turn to face Cooper.

I say, 'Gilby is hurting Elsie and he's hurting other kids too.'

And there – IT'S OUT!

We look at one another. Cooper looks different - relieved, somehow.

'I know,' he says.

'We have to do something.'

Cooper nods.

I say, 'Come to my house after school.'

We reach the school gates and go our separate ways.

I try to concentrate on lessons. Elsie is quiet and avoids eye contact. Juna is a shadow and I can feel her hovering. At break, Gilby is never far away. You can hear his mean voice in the corridors, even if you can't see him.

Miss Askew takes registration and now I know she's leaving to go far away, I feel sad. It feels strange being the only one in the class who knows she's going to Rwanda.

When the final bell rings there's a scramble to get outside. Gilby hangs around the gates, but Elsie and I merge into the crowd and manage to slip past him.

Elsie is very quiet. When we reach the Box Brownie café, she says, 'See you later, Ellie,' but she doesn't look at me.

'Bye,' I say.

It's been a while since Elsie and I did our homework

together, or had a proper chat. It's difficult to talk to her now. It's as though we're not friends at all.

I head off home feeling miserable and lonely.

I think about Jack. His advice was to tell someone that Gilby is a bully. The telling bit isn't easy – but at least I've told Cooper.

Grandma and Nanna are in the kitchen. I notice there's an awkward silence.

I say, 'Cooper's coming round.'

Nanna says, 'A boy? Why?'

Her question makes me feel guilty, but I don't know why.

I say, 'To talk… about school… the play.' I realise I'm in that grey area, where honesty is difficult and truth is blurred.

But Grandma says, 'You can go in the den and I'll bring you snacks.' She gives Nanna a weary look.

I could kiss Grandma. I feel sorry that Nanna sometimes makes her life a misery. Grandma is easy-going. With Nanna, it's her way or no way.

Nanna says, to no one in particular, 'She shouldn't eat between meals. She'll spoil her appetite.'

Grandma winks at me. 'Off you go, Ellie,' she says.

I change out of my uniform and put on jeans and a warm woolly jumper. I stand by the window and watch for Cooper. It's almost dark and it's raining hard. I see him hurrying along the promenade and turn up the hill. Silly boy – he's not wearing a coat! I run downstairs and let him in.

Cooper steps inside, shivering and dripping wet. I call for Grandma. When she sees him, she's concerned. She calls,

'Eddie!' and bundles Cooper upstairs. Eddie runs after them. I hear Cooper coughing. When he comes down, his hair is towelled dry and he's wearing a pair of Eddie's jeans and one of his jumpers. I think he has a pair of Eddie's socks on too. Grandma takes his shoes to dry in the kitchen. He looks embarrassed.

We go into the den. Fin is doing a Gruffalo jigsaw on the floor and when he sees Cooper, he pounces and tries to wrestle him, like he does with Eddie and Dad. Then Grandma comes back with mugs of tomato soup, a basket of dippy bread and a packet of dried apricots for Fin. Suddenly, there's no better place to be in the whole wide world, than in this warm, messy room.

Cooper says, 'Your grandma's really nice.'

I nod.

We help Fin with his jigsaw and I tell Cooper about Elsie's bruise and how she won't let me tell anyone because she's afraid Cadence might get stressed and want to sell the café – and how Juna banged her head when Gilby Flynn pushed her against the wall.

Cooper tells me he saw Gilby grab Elsie, so now he watches him to keep her safe – and that's why he missed his doctor's appointment.

Cooper eyes are ringed with dark circles. He's wheezy and he coughs.

I say, 'You shouldn't smoke, Cooper.'

He shrugs. 'I've quit. Can't afford to, anyway.'

I say, 'Good. Well, you should wear a coat then. Keep yourself warm.'

'You sound like your grandma,' he says.

There's an awkward silence. Cooper concentrates on Fin's jigsaw.

Then he says 'I don't have a coat.'

There's another silence while I absorb this. It's hard to imagine not having a coat, especially in winter.

'It got nicked,' he says, 'so I've got to keep out of my old man's way. He's got a bit of a temper.'

'Why would he be angry?' I ask. 'Wouldn't he just buy you another one?'

Cooper pulls a sort of smile. 'He's not what you call the *generous* type,' he says.

This is a shock, though I know there are poor families, and I know there are families with problems. I realise, with a sick feeling, that Cooper's father is probably nothing like my dad who, irritating as he is, would never allow me to be cold.

Mum comes in to get Fin, who wants to stay. Fin grabs Cooper's legs and won't let go, which makes Cooper laugh – and I think: *I've never heard you laugh before.*

Mum says, 'Be a good boy and come and eat your tea. You can see Cooper later.'

Grandma comes in with dishes of risotto. I realise I am quite hungry.

We sit on the floor and eat. I tell Cooper about the red letters I've seen from the lighthouse, and how they spell SLIME. And how I called Gilby a SLIMY LITTLE SUCKER, which makes Cooper laugh again, and we high five one another.

Then I remember the 9-H poster in my pocket – so I get it

and show it to him.

Cooper nods and says, 'Did you see the one yesterday - 10-T? They're all over. Tied to trees, in bus shelters, on lamp posts.'

'What do they mean?' I ask.

Cooper says, 'If there's one tomorrow that says 8-something, it might be a countdown to zero.'

I'm impressed. I hadn't thought of that. Herman barges the door open with his head and Fin toddles in to say goodnight. Cooper high-fives him, but Fin wants a hug. Tonight, for some reason, Fin seems quite sweet.

Eddie offers to drive Cooper home and hands him one of his winter jackets.

'Any use?' asks Eddie, simply.

Cooper says, 'Sure,' and puts it on. He's embarrassed but mostly relieved, I think. He looks at his feet and mutters, 'Thanks.'

Grandma has dried Cooper's things and hands them to him in a big bag, stuffed with more of Eddie's clothes. She gives a little smile. It's funny how Grandma knows things without even being told. She's sort of magic sometimes.

As they're going out, Eddie says, 'You've got an email, Ellie. The laptop's on the table.'

I go into the kitchen.

I read:

FROM: Jack Bell
TO: Menella Booton
SUBJECT: School play

Hi Ellie
R U OK? Have you told about Gilby?
I'm visiting Auntie Maggie and will arrive on Friday night
next week. I can see the play on Saturday.
C U then.
Jack
PS Any more red letters?

I write back:

Hi Jack
Yes, I have told someone about Gilby. I'm glad you're coming
to visit, though don't expect much from the play. Things
aren't going to plan. Let's just say, it's not going to make the
West End.

Grandma has seen the lighthouse letters too. So far we've
seen: S-L-I-M-E. I'm pretty sure Gilby is behind it.

I think about telling Jack that Miss Askew is going to
Rwanda and that she doesn't like to show her feelings – but
Susannah said this was a secret, so I write:

I'll look out for more red letters.

I click SEND.

I go to my bedroom and sit in the dark. From the
lighthouse, there's a sudden red beam of light. After a few
moments U, then C, then K, flash in the dark. Then there's

nothing – just the usual white light sweeping round and round.

I hurry to Grandma's sitting room.

She says, 'More letters!'

Grandma picks up a pen and a brown envelope. She's already written:

M – L – I – E – S, and she adds, U – C – K.

Grandma says, 'What other words can I see? Hmm. LIKES, LUCK and LICKS.

I study the letters. I can see: MUCK, SICK and SCUM.

Grandma looks worried. She says, 'My, my. How gloomy! Your glass needs topping up, my girl. It's half-empty.'

I sort of know what she means. Grandma is a glass half-full person. But I'm not. Not any more.

I go back to my room. It strikes me that nobody I know is perfectly happy or has a perfect family. Mum is tired and sick of Dad. Dad is frazzled with himself and his silly book. It's hard to be happy around Nanna and Gramps who always bicker. Cadence divorced Elsie's dad and now it looks like she doesn't want Jem in her life - and Jem doesn't want her. And Cooper would rather freeze than tell his dad about his stolen coat.

Grandma always thinks that everything will work out just fine. I hope she's right, but I'm not holding my breath.

WEDNESDAY - 8

I don't expect Elsie to be waiting for me at the Box Brownie café – and she isn't. No disappointment there. I wave at Cadence, pull a fake smile and hurry past. Further down the promenade there's a new poster taped up in the shelter and others are tied to lamp posts with green stripy string.

Today's poster says:

8
E

I tug one off, fold it, and put it in my pocket. I hurry up the hill and meet Cooper at the usual spot. He has a poster in his hand.

'There's loads of them,' he says. 'They're all along the street. People are starting to get curious.'

I say, 'You're right. It *is* a countdown.'

'Unless the letters are scrambled, the first word seems to be *the.*'

'The *what?*' I ask.

Cooper shrugs. 'We'll know when it gets to zero, next Thursday.'

'That's the first performance of the play,' I say. 'You don't think they're linked, do you?'

We look at one another, alarmed.

'I guess we'll find out,' says Cooper.

He pulls up the collar of Eddie's old jacket and digs his hands into the pockets, like he's been wearing it for years. It's his jacket now and I'm glad. At least he's warm.

I say, 'I saw more red letters flashed from the lighthouse last night. U, C, K. Grandma saw them too.'

'What time?' he asks.

'A few minutes after you left. You must have just missed them.'

We walk in silence. I can almost hear Cooper's brain whirring round – and I can definitely hear mine.

'I'll call round tonight,' he says at the school gate, and he disappears into the crowd.

Miss Askew is ÜBER stressed. It seems everyone in the cast has a sore throat or a cough, and at the lunchtime rehearsal, the chorus line of abandoned kids sounds more like the lost goat variety. *Not* good!

Miss Askew looks more beige than usual.

'For goodness sake!' she screeches. 'Eat lots of oranges and get to bed early. **That's an order!** Otherwise, when I leave this school, a brass plaque will go up in the foyer saying: *Thank goodness, Miss Askew's GONE!'*

Someone sneezes. Miss Askew flaps her arms like a penguin.

She squawks, 'Coughs and sneezes spread diseases. If

you don't have a tissue, sneeze into your arm.' She demonstrates. 'We can't have the cast going down with flu. If you catch it, I don't care *how* you feel. **YOU TURN UP AND *SING!*'**

This is definitely not Miss Askew's worst day, or even one close to it, so you can imagine what a pain she's been.

I think: *Well, at least she's starting to show her feelings.*

She looks and sounds worried, upset, anxious and stressed – all at the same time. And I can't escape her - she's my form teacher - so maybe you can understand how I've become a glass half-empty kinda kid?

Elsie is a nervous wreck. She's more or less stopped talking or even making eye contact, though that doesn't stop her singing like an angel. Juna Budd is a creepy shadow hauling round her skull and crossbones bag. Abigail Jennings turns up at rehearsals to pick at her nails and give Elsie the evil eye, popping out now and then to have a secret cig - and Gilby Flynn can be sensed everywhere, dispensing his nasty brand of meanness. When he sings, he hits the right notes but still manages to sound ugly.

Because I'm Miss Askew's Assistant, (with a capital A) she's started confiding in me, in unexpected ways.

She mutters things like, 'They'll *pay* me to get on a plane out of here.'

I'm not sure what to say. I shuffle scripts, or I look at the floor and sometimes I nod sympathetically. When she eyeballs me, I say things like: *It's going well, Miss Askew… It will be fine on the night, Miss Askew… You're doing a great job, Miss Askew…*

Elsie has a dentist's appointment, so she disappears ten minutes before the school bell. LUCKY HER. I trudge out of school, too tired to even think about Gilby. BIG mistake. When I get to the gates, he's there like a giant spider and Juna is trapped in his web.

He says, 'Tuna should be mixed with mayonnaise and *mashed up*. Mmm. Spread nice and thick on a piece of bread.'

His minions giggle. I don't think I'll ever eat tuna again. Juna tries to dodge past him but he sidesteps and blocks her.

Then he sees me and shouts, 'Here comes BOOTS, stinking of VOMIT, as usual.'

I look at his feet. He's wearing ankle boots with fancy silver buckles.

I say, 'Now, that's what you call a pair of boots.' And then I take a closer look. It just so happens, he's standing in a big pile of dog poo.

Everyone around the gate looks - what's the word? AGHAST. Mouths drop open in disgust.

Gilby is humiliated and that makes him *angry*. He takes a step towards me. I grab Juna by the hand, just as Cooper strides through the gate, swinging his bag onto his shoulder which swipes Gilby in the chest. It's enough to knock him sideways. There's a chorus of nervous giggles as Gilby staggers, trying to keep his balance.

'Oops. Sorry mate,' says Cooper gruffly, but we keep going and we don't look back.

It's strange to be walking with Cooper *and* Juna. She's not a talker, that's for sure. When we get to the top of Curly

Lane, she peels off and walks away. I look after her in disbelief. Cooper and I practically saved her life and she doesn't even say thank you. Suddenly, she turns round. She stands and looks at us for the longest minute. I start to feel embarrassed. Then she calls, 'Thanks!'

I've been brought up to be polite. I call back, 'Any time,' and want to kick myself. OH NO! Juna thinks I can fight her battles for her. Haven't I enough problems?

'Gilby's going to peg me out to dry,' I say miserably.

'Just let him try,' says Cooper.

At 6:31 the doorbell rings. It's Cooper looking warm in a jumper and jacket and Grandma smiles when she sees him. He's brought his school bag, so we sit at the table, not talking, and do some homework. I've already eaten, but Grandma puts snacks on the table.

Cooper says, 'Thank you,' and quietly munches his way through a chunk of Cheddar cheese and crackers, a couple of fat gherkins and a pickled onion, an apple and a big slice of chocolate cake, without even taking his eyes off his homework. Then he notices I'm stuck on algebra, so he corrects my mistake and explains it better than my maths teacher.

It's dawning on me that Cooper is pretty smart.

Grandma goes to read in her sitting room. Nanna comes into the kitchen and stands in the corner watching us for a while, then she sniffs and goes away.

Cooper suddenly says, 'I wish Gilby would just go away.'

'Well that would solve one problem,' I say. Then I think:

But what about the play?

The first performance is next Thursday night. There's another on Friday and two on Saturday, and then – it's over. Miss Askew is bowing out of our school - and she'll be gone - maybe forever. What's more, there's no guarantee that the play will be any good at all. It's easy to see why she's STRESSED.

All this adds up to a worry that's like a tricky algebra problem:

If:

G = GILBY

- teachers are fooled by Gilby's toothpaste smile and his fake party manners – so he flies UNDER the radar of suspicion – but the truth is, he's sly and secretive and bullies just about every kid in school who wears glasses, or has red hair, or an unusual name, or isn't good at sports, or isn't very tall, or is this or isn't that.

And if:

P = PLAY

- which is Miss Askew's very LAST production at this school and she's gone to the trouble of writing it herself. It's what Dad would call her swan song.*

And if:

T = TELLING TEACHERS ABOUT GILBY

- which will result in Gilby being excluded from school, with a bit of luck.

Then:

T (telling) = P (play) minus G (Gilby)

And:

P (play) minus G (Gilby) = F (flop)

$$T = P - G$$

$$P - G = F$$

*- because Gilby's understudy, Cody Child, chickened out ages ago – so there's no one to play Charlie. The play will flop. Miss Askew will leave our school feeling a **BFF**, and in this case, that means a BIG FAT FAILURE.*

But:

P (play) + G (Gilby) = M (misery)

*- because Gilby will keep bullying Elsie and Juna and all the other kids that he pushes around behind the scenes. And I'm pretty MISERABLE too, because I'm sure it's just a matter of time before Gilby turns me into some sort of equation. It's what's called a **NO WIN SITUATION.** In my head I feel a big, silent: AAAARRRRRGGGGHHHHH! And what's worse – most of the above equals a SECRET.*

And I think: ***SECRETS are sometimes REALLY BAD – I mean, ROTTEN TO THE CORE.***

Then I remember something Susannah said: that the secret about Miss Askew isn't a *total* secret, because it's shared with trusted people.

I look at Cooper, and it's funny to realise - not in a ha ha way, and not in a weird way – but in a nice surprise way – that I *trust* him.

'Cooper...' I say.

Then... Eddie barges in from the workshop and picks up his car keys. He crams a biscuit into his mouth, looks at the clock and says, 'Nuts!'

I think crossly: *What a scruff he is, with his messy hair and his torn clothes. And why can't he EVER be on time?*

Spitting crumbs he says, 'I'll drop you off at the end of Curly Lane if you want, Coop. I'm late, so we need to scram.'

Cooper sweeps his books into his bag, grabs his coat and disappears after Eddie.

I stare at the door, unable to believe Cooper could just run off like that.

I think: *Cadence is right. You can't count on any man and that's the truth.* I pack up my books and go to my room. I sit in the dark watching the lighthouse for a long time.

Nothing unusual to report.

THURSDAY - 7

Have you ever heard the saying – to get out of bed on the wrong side? Well, that's what I did this morning.

Everything is WRONG. I feel *really* fed up!

I am fed up with GILBY because he is such a nasty piece of work. I am fed up with Elsie because she puts up with Gilby rather than telling someone about him. I am fed up with Mum and Dad because they're miserable together. I am fed up with Eddie, because he's a lousy boyfriend to Susannah - always scruffy and late. And *most* of all, I am *fed up* with COOPER!

Why did I think he was worth one *minute* of my time?

It's windy and cold. I don't bother to fasten my coat. I trudge down the hill. I don't bother to look in the window of the Box Brownie café. I walk past with my head down. Why should I care about Elsie if she doesn't care about herself?

The seagulls keep me company. They screech and circle. Waves thud on the beach. The more noise the better.

I shout: 'I'M FED UP WITH THE LOT OF YOU!'

I go past the end lamp post, and there's another poster flapping madly in the wind.

It says:

7

F

Big deal! So what? I reach the other side of the cove and start the climb into town.

Roll on Christmas. Roll on the day when I can leave this school forever. Roll on when I can leave this town and *everybody* in it.

Behind me, I hear Cooper shout, '**ELLIE!**'

I ignore him and keep walking as fast as I can.

Another call, '**ELLIE, WAIT!**'

If I were an Olympic sprinter, I would cruise up the hill.

'**HANG ON!**' he cries.

I hear Cooper huffing and puffing, hauling his bag stuffed with text books.

He says, 'I guess you didn't hear me.'

'Say goodbye last night? No I guess I didn't,' I say crossly.

We fall into step. I keep my eyes on the ground.

Cooper says, 'Sorry...' I shrug my shoulders. 'I just had this mad idea that I might find out who's behind the lighthouse letters.'

'*What?*' I say.

'I couldn't tell you in front of Eddie, could I? He dropped me off and I doubled back and ran across the fields to the lighthouse.'

'Well, there weren't any letters last night,' I say, coolly.

'True,' he says, 'but someone went *into* the lighthouse.'

I stop and look at him.

'Who?' I ask.

Cooper looks worried. He puts his hand on my shoulder.

I must be slipping. I didn't sense that slug, Gilby, slithering towards me.

Gilby sings at the top of his voice: 'SMELLY AND POOPER SITTING IN A TREE, K-I-S-S-I-N-G.'

There's hoots of laughter. Then his minions join in.

Cooper says, 'How sweet. You've learned a new nursery rhyme. What's up, Gilby? You look uncomfortable. Is it time for a nappy change?'

Gilby's not sure what to say.

He manages, 'You're the pooper, Cooper. At least I haven't got a girlfriend called Smelly Boots.'

Cooper says flatly, 'Grow up.'

We turn away in disgust and walk on, but it's pretty *horrible* when there's a trail of sniggering kids taunting you. It's true. Some kids are GROSS.

At the school gates, Cooper gives me a hunted look, then he goes one way and I go another.

Lunchtime rehearsal. Miss Askew is making a big effort to stay calm, but it's easy to see that she's tired and stressed. Everyone is here except Gilby Flynn who is late, as usual. Elsie stands centre stage looking pale and unhappy.

Miss Askew checks her watch for the tenth time. Gilby swaggers on stage with a smirk on his face.

Miss Askew says, 'At last. Mr Flynn graces us with his presence. I'm sure you've been doing something very important. Organising World Peace perhaps? If that's the case, I have no problem with your lateness.'

There's an awkward silence, but I quite enjoy this one. It's time Miss Askew got tough with Gilby.

She does her jug impression. 'Well?' she demands.

Gilby shakes his head.

'Then your tardiness disrespects me *and* the cast. You need these people to support your performance. It's not smart to alienate them.'

I think: *Jeepers! If only she knew...*

Gilby smirks at his minions, who will need to look up the word *alienate* in a dictionary, and probably *tardiness* and *disrespect* too.

She says firmly, 'One week to go before the first performance. Everyone should know the songs and their lines. No ifs, no buts. We'll run through scenes without stopping. If you mess up – you carry on.'

There's a chorus of nervous whispers.

She says, 'Sorry – but that's how it is. We're on a *countdown*!'

Countdown! Cooper and I exchange looks. He hovers at the side of the stage ready to shift the scenery.

Gilby sneers at Cooper but Cooper watches him steadily and stays calm. Gilby turns round and sees me. I hold my chin up and look at him without blinking. This is the message, Gilby: *You're not watching us - WE are WATCHING YOU!*

Gilby goes red and shifts uncomfortably in his snazzy boots. Elsie stares at the floor, like she's blocked everything out. Everyone is quiet. I scan faces and see Juna huddled with the waifs and strays at the far side of the stage. She looks at me and gives a small smile. I don't think I've ever seen her smile before.

Miss Askew folds her arms and looks over her glasses.

'Right. LET'S GO FOR IT… *Cue music!*'

Rehearsal does *not* go well. Elsie looks sad and sounds sad (even through the happy songs) and by the end of the run-through, I feel like I need counselling.

What cheers me up and bothers me at the same time, is that Gilby keeps messing up. For such a *confident* bully, he suddenly seems uncertain. The play can't happen without him – but *with* him is almost as bad. He forgets his lines, hits some bum notes and starts to sulk. His minions, who always hang round him, look sheepish. Miss Askew wrings her hands.

She mutters, 'This is the way the world ends. Not with a bang, but a whimper.'*

The final bell rings. I wait outside the staff room to collect the revised timetable of rehearsals. From tomorrow, there's going to be two – one at lunchtime and one after school. Miss Askew appears and gives me a pile of photocopies.

She says, 'You're a good little helper, Ellie Booton. I'm going to miss you.'

Before I can say anything, she turns around and she's gone.

School has emptied out. When I get to the school gates, I

think I'm in the clear. I'm wrong. Gilby steps out from behind the wall.

In a mean voice he says, 'You better watch it, Smelly.'

Watch what? I'm distracted by a spot on his eyelid that looks swollen and painful. His eye is red and watery.

I wait patiently for him to say more, but I'm tired. *Poor* Miss Askew, I think. And *who* did Cooper see going into the lighthouse? And *why* doesn't Elsie wait for me any more?

'What should I watch? Spit it out then,' I say.

He gets that stage fright look again.

'Just watch it, that's all,' he says feebly. He slings his bag on his shoulder and turns to cross the road, then looks back and says nastily, 'Or you'll be sorry.'

He steps into the road, in front of a car. The driver slams on her brakes and he yelps and jumps back.

NEAR MISS!

On the other side of the road I see Abigail Jennings. She's waiting for a boy who can't be trusted to cross the road by himself. *Not cool.*

I feel shaken up. My heart is beating really fast. I'm halfway down the hill when I see Elsie sitting in a bus shelter. She sees me and waves. I run the rest of the way, though my legs are wobbly.

'Thanks for waiting,' I say, handing her one of the photocopies. 'This will cheer you up. Two rehearsals every day from now on.'

'Oh goodie,' she says, flatly.

A little green van comes up the hill and does a right turn

into town. On the side of the van, in gold letters it says: *Jeremy Hardy – Greengrocer, Fruitier & Purveyor of Fine Foods.*

It's Jem and in the passenger seat is Jack's auntie, Maggie Bell, laughing her head off. *Miss* Maggie Bell: *single,* professional, *attractive,* with a good sense of humour.

And that, as Dad would say, puts the cherry on the parfait.*

Elsie and I look at one another. We're both thinking the same thing: *Maggie is now Jem's girlfriend and Cadence, Elsie's mum... ISN'T.* She's been dropped like a stone a week before her fortieth birthday. Elsie looks hurt and shakes her head.

'You can't count on any man, *and that's the truth,*' she says.

I get home and go to my bedroom. I try to do my homework but I just can't concentrate. Grandma says my special gift is being able to think outside the box and ask questions that no one has thought to ask – but what's the point of asking questions when there are no answers?

Why is Gilby such a rotten bully? Why has Jem gone off with laugh-a-lot Maggie, when Cadence is so lovely? Will Mum and Dad *ever* be happy again?

I hear the telephone.

Eddie yells up the stairs, 'Cooper's on the phone.'

Then Dad, with his flappy ears, opens his office door and calls, quite rudely, 'Make it snappy. I'm expecting a call.'

Eddie disappears into the workshop. I wait until I hear

Dad shut his door. At least there's one question that can be answered: *who went into the lighthouse?*

I run downstairs, pick up the phone and say, 'Who *was* it?'

Cooper ignores me.

He says, 'I had to dash off. Did you get home all right?'

I say, 'Gilby was waiting for me. He told me to watch it, or I'd be sorry – then he nearly got hit by a car.'

'Geez,' says Cooper. 'We've got to report him, Ellie.'

'I know,' I say. 'But P minus G equals F.'

'What?'

'*Play* minus *Gilby* equals *flop*. If Gilby gets excluded, what will happen to the play?'

There's a silence. Cooper knows just as much as I do that Cody has given up. The play will have to be cancelled.

'Flippin' marvellous,' says Cooper flatly.

There's another silence. It's not awkward. Our thoughts collide. We come to the same conclusion.

Cooper sighs. 'We'll watch him. We'll get through the play – then we'll report him. Agreed?'

'Agreed,' I say. It feels like a plan, at least. 'What happened to you, anyway?' I ask.

'I went to see the doctor.'

Poor Cooper, I think. He's not well.

'Have you got some medicine?' I ask.

'Antibiotics. I'll soon be fixed. Anyway…,' he takes a deep breath. 'This might not be the news you expected.'

I say, 'O-K?' because I have *no idea* what to expect.

'Are you on your own?'

I hear something behind me, but it's only Herman coming down the stairs and I'd trust him with any information.

'Yes.' I can hear my heart beating.

Cooper whispers, 'It was Eddie.'

'*EDDIE?!*'

'Shh. He had a key. He took a bag out of the boot of his car, took it inside, came out and drove off. It only took a minute.'

Mum comes out of the den with the Finster who whacks me on the legs with his Star Wars lightsaber.

'Accident!' laughs Fin.

It *so* was *not*.

Mum says, 'Come and set the table, Ellie.'

I take a deep breath. I feel like my head might pop off - but if it does, it might hit Fin as hard as he's just hit me.

'Uh-huh. I'd better go,' I say. 'I'll meet you on the way to school.'

I put the phone down. Mum looks at me with a big question in her eyes. What's so interesting about me having a phone call from Cooper anyway?

I say, 'The play. It's a nightmare.'

Mum nods.

I feel GUILTY. Not telling *quite* the truth is a very tricky business.

FRIDAY - 6

At least it isn't raining. You see – I'm still capable of being a glass half-full kinda kid. On the other hand – maybe I'm not, because I feel like there's a huge storm on the horizon. It can only get worse. I pass the Box Brownie café and head along the promenade. There's lots of noise in the air all jumbled together: wind, seagulls, sea. Someone taps my shoulder and I nearly jump out of my skin. It's Elsie.

'Sorry,' she says. 'I waved but you didn't see me.'

We're hit by a blast of wind which blows my hood down, whipping hair across my face. We run into a shelter. I put my bag down and drag my hair into a scrunchie. Elsie fishes something out of her pocket – the scrap of red and yellow checked fabric.

She says, 'I know somebody who wears a shirt made out of this.'

She looks at me like I might want to guess, but I really, *really* don't.

'Eddie!' she says. I feel a bit dizzy. 'Are you all right, Ellie?'

I think: *Grandma is WRONG. I can't think outside the box for TOFFEE!*

I say, 'Cooper saw Eddie going into the lighthouse with a

bag. And the red letters make some really weird words – like SICK and SCUM and SLIME.'

Elsie looks pretty horrified.

I really don't like the idea that Eddie is doing something wrong. He's my brother, after all.

We hurry along the promenade and on alternate lamp posts, tied with stripy string, are new posters which say:

6
A

All these clues! What do they mean?

Cooper's waiting at the top of Curly Lane. He gives me a look, and I know what he's thinking: *Is it OK to talk in front of Elsie?*

So I say, 'Elsie knows everything – and the bit of material we found stuck on the lighthouse gate might be from Eddie's shirt.'

Elsie pulls it out of her pocket and shows Cooper.

He nods and says, 'He wears that shirt all the time. It's torn as well.'

I think: *Why didn't I recognise it? I must see it practically EVERY DAY, except when it crawls by itself to the washer, like his other clothes have to. What's happening to me?*

Cooper looks at me. 'Familiarity breeds contempt,' he says.

'What the heck does that mean?' I ask.

'It means,' he says gently, 'that when you see something *every* day, you stop noticing it.'

We pass a bus shelter. Inside, there are lots of the 6-A posters stuck on the glass with tape and further up the road, others tied to lamp posts.

Cooper rips one down.

He says, 'But someone is desperate for these to be noticed.'

'They're crazy,' says Elsie.

'It's a countdown with a letter every day. So far: T,H,E and F,A,' I say.

'The… something,' says Elsie. 'What? Fact? Family? Farm?'

'We'll know by zero,' says Cooper.

We hear Gilby's mean voice behind us. He's walking alongside Juna, getting in her face and bumping her roughly with his shoulder.

Juna walks with her head down, even when Gilby shoves her into a prickly hedge. I see her more clearly now. She's like a shadow because she's so pale and thin. I look at Elsie. She's pale too. I think she may have lost weight.

I don't know why, but I suddenly feel tall, though I'm pretty sure I haven't grown that much since I got up this morning. I look at Cooper.

Together, we turn and walk towards Juna. Elsie hesitates, but tags on.

Cooper shouts at the top of his voice, *'JUNA!'*

She looks up. Her expression shocks me. It's a complicated mix of relief and fear, hope and despair. I never noticed before how lonely she is.

Gilby looks less sure of himself as we stride towards him.

His minions materialise out of nowhere. I find myself preoccupied with how many spots they all have, and wonder who would win the trophy for the school's most unattractive boy. To be fair, they'd all be in with a good chance.

Gilby says, 'Picking up strays, Pooper? The ginger tom -' he looks at Elsie '- the moggie -' he jerks his head towards Juna '- and the prissy Persian.'

I guess I'm the prissy Persian.

'Toms are male, you idiot,' says Cooper. 'I respect cats though. They're independent and they have claws.'

Gilby laughs, nervously. 'Aw,' he says, 'little kitties don't worry me.' He tries to give Juna another shove but Cooper blocks him. Cooper seems taller too. He leans into Gilby's face.

'Bullying girls. You're an embarrassment, mate,' he says.

At this point, Juna and Elsie hold their heads up. They have to – it's so intense – and I see more than before.

Bullies don't have friends! They have so-called mates who hang round, hoping for a bit of excitement – because they're pathetic and their lives are empty. And these *mates* don't want to back the losing side because that would make them more pathetic. At this point, Cooper is pretty convincing and Gilby looks like a fool. Cooper's surrounded by girls – they're just boys who *wish* they were surrounded by girls.

I'm anxious, but I say in a calm voice, 'Come on. Don't want to be late.'

We turn our backs on them and walk away.

I say to Juna, 'We'll hang round together.'

Juna nods. She's very pale, but she smiles and says, 'OK.'

Another *troubled* rehearsal.

'***Good grief!***' screeches Miss Askew.

For a woman who doesn't like to show her emotions, she's doing great, but maybe not in a good way.

'We have to end the play on an ***upbeat note***,' she cries, 'otherwise the Samaritans will be overwhelmed with calls from folk saying: *I've just endured a school play that's taken away my **REASON TO LIVE!***'

You don't need me to tell you that she's not in a good place right now. Her hands go on her hips. Her head tips to one side. She studies us with her small button eyes.

'Do you ***want*** folk to go home in ***despair?***' she demands.

Even Gilby shakes his head.

'Well then, **PICK IT UP!** You do a fantastic job of sounding SAD in the sad bits – but when the $HAPPY$ **BITS** start - *for the love of all that is* $SACRED$, **PLEASE - SOUND –** *HAPPY!*'

Miss Askew is losing it more or less every rehearsal now. It's like she's on the brink of realising that she's *NO* Pavarotti – that she can't even be trusted to teach Happy Birthday to a bunch of toddlers. What's *happened* to her? She needs to go out with a bang, otherwise how will her new school introduce her?

'Boys and girls, please welcome Miss Askew, our new teacher, who is completely *LOUSY* at producing school plays.'

I definitely feel sorry for Miss Askew, but I *don't* feel sorry for Gilby who seems to be going to pieces. It's strange to witness, because when the spotlight's on him and he's got to show a bit of *real* talent (other than being a first-class bully) – he's got nothing to give.

Abigail, Elsie's mean-girl understudy, has a cold and after every secret cigarette break, she comes back stinking like Fag Ash Lil (as Grandma would say) with an ugly, wheezy cough. So, you might as well write her off, because a flu infected frog would sing better.

Cody, Gilby's understudy, has stopped coming to rehearsals altogether and when I see him in the corridor he limps (sometimes on one foot, sometimes on the other) and he avoids eye contact. He's determined not to get into a tangle with Gilby and any excuse will do. In other words, he's completely *bottled* it.

The pressure is ALL on Elsie and Gilby and it's mounting. I didn't know show business could be this tough. I can honestly say I'm *relieved* I'm not in the play, and I'm definitely *glad* I'm not directing it, especially since the reviews will probably stink. Poor Miss Askew. I think she's right. It looks like she *will* go out with a whimper.

The after-school rehearsal goes much the same. Afterwards, we see Gilby slither into his dad's set of wheels – a new black BMW with smoked glass windows. These are pricey cars because my dad has an old one and is planning to get a new one if he ever wins the lottery. I start to walk home with Cooper, Juna and Elsie.

Cooper lives on the same side of town as Juna, so they go off together. Elsie and I carry on down the hill and reach the promenade. It's been a bleak day, but the sight of the Box Brownie in the distance, all twinkly and pink, makes it seem more normal somehow.

Cadence is closing the café as we reach it. When she sees us, her mouth smiles but her eyes don't.

'Had a good day?' she asks.

'Fine, Mum,' says Elsie and shoots me a look.

I'm getting really good at reading looks.

I say, 'Yes, fine. Everything's all right. Almost perfect, in fact.' Then I give a big, cheesy grin.

Cadence eyes me suspiciously, because I'm no good at lying. It's not a talent I want to cultivate and anyway, to be *perfectly honest*, I'm pretty DESPERATE to tell the truth.

I say goodbye and walk home.

When I open the front door, Herman's there, smiling and wagging his tail as usual. I hear Dad on the phone in his ivory tower. I go into the kitchen. There's a message on the whiteboard in Mum's writing: *Taken Nanna and Gramps shopping. Back later.*

I feel irritated. Of course they'll be back later! They can't come back before they've gone, can they? I wander into the workshop to see if Grandma and Eddie are around. It's deserted. Herman pads after me and starts following his nose. He sniffs out a spider and stuffs his head under a workbench to say hello. It dawns on me that this is a perfect opportunity to have a good sniff round too. Eddie works on a bench at the far end of the workshop, underneath a big skylight. It's always a mess, but there's nothing hidden or sinister – just like Eddie. I feel relieved. But then, tucked away on the bottom shelf, I see a bulky, black plastic sack. I pull it out and expect it to be heavy, but it's not. I study the way it's tied, then untie it. Inside there are large rectangular tiles with the shape of a letter cut out of each one. I shake them out of the bag.

The cut-out letters are: G, O, D, W, A.

These tiles would be perfect for shining a light through, to make the glowing lighthouse letters.

Herman pricks up his ears and wags his tail. Someone is coming! I quickly put the tiles back in the bag, tie it in the same way, and stuff it back on the shelf. Herman disappears to do his meet and greet duty. I duck down.

I see Eddie's feet in his scruffy trainers walk towards me. I'm on my hands and knees on the dusty workshop floor, hiding from my own brother! *WHAT IS HAPPENING?*

At his workbench, Eddie tears open a brown envelope, reads something, then tosses it aside. Herman pads back into the workshop, sniffs me out and comes over to give me a lick. I think the game's up, but then Eddie farts and laughs. Herman is distracted by the whiff. I pinch my nose. Why is it that boys with trumpet trousers find it funny, when it's just *embarrassing* – not to mention, *anti-social?* He fishes in his pocket, opens a drawer in the bench, takes out a small tin and drops something in it with a metallic clang. He puts the tin back, closes the drawer and goes out of the room.

Herman stays put, staring at me as if to say: *What are you doing, Ellie?*

I wait for a minute. All's quiet. I sneak over to Eddie's bench and open the drawer. I open the tin and take out a key. Tied to it with string is a worn paper tag that says: LIGHTHOUSE. I gasp. This confirms it. My brother is involved. I put the key back and close the drawer.

I hurry up to my bedroom, grab a pen and write down the new letters in my notebook.

What I already know are: S, L, I, M, E and U, C, K, and now I've found the cut-out letters G, O, D, W, A.

Should I tell Grandma that Eddie's the one going into the lighthouse – that he's the one who is making the letters? And what words do the letters make now?

Straight away, I can see GOD, DOG and DUCK.

I think: *Does GOD know that I've been spying on my brother? Did he see me DUCK down with my DOG?*

Am I going *crazy?*

Then, in the new letters I see *GOAD,* and that's definitely another Gilby-type word.

Friday night has always been my most favourite time of the week because after I've worked hard at school, I have the whole weekend ahead of me. But tonight I feel ÜBER, ÜBER, *ÜBER* STRESSED. To cap it all, Eddie shouts up the stairs to tell me that Susannah is busy and can't give me a guitar lesson. This is very bad news. I really need to see Susannah.

I stand at the top of the stairs and call down, 'Why?'

'Secret stuff,' shouts Eddie.

'What secret stuff?'

But Eddie looks up, taps his nose in a very *irritating* way, goes out of the house and drives off.

Mum and Fin finally get home with Nanna and Gramps. They've had fish and chips in town because Nanna and Gramps have to eat at five o'clock, on the dot. Mum has a headache. Without a word, she hands the Finster to Dad, takes two paracetamol and goes to bed.

Dad looks annoyed. He asks me what I want for tea. I would like *chish* and *fips* too (that's what I call them) but Dad's lost his sense of humour and says it's something on toast – like it or lump it.

I say, 'Why ask me then, if I don't have a choice?'

Dad says crossly, 'That's enough lip from you m'lady.'

'I don't want anything,' I say.

'Manners?' snaps Dad.

'I don't want anything, THANK YOU VERY MUCH.'

I hurry back to my room and close the door with a little bit of a slam.

I settle on my window seat under my knitted woolly blanket. It's dark except for the lighthouse beam sweeping round. There's nothing out there but empty dark space, chilled air and choppy sea. It's completely bleak and so am I.

Car lights come into view. The security light pops on. It's Grandma. She parks on the drive and hauls a bag out of the boot.

I run down the stairs to meet her. I open the door and a blast of wind practically blows her inside and wafts a lovely smell of food. We bump into one another. I wrap my arms round her tightly. I can always rely on Grandma.

She says 'Chish and fips for supper.'

We eat in Grandma's sitting room. Everything around Grandma is cosy. I realise it's been quite a while since I've had a cosy time with Mum. I can't *ever* remember having a cosy time with Dad. He's always working. He needs *space* to think, he needs *space* to write, and he needs *space* to think about his writing.

I say, 'Is Mum ill, Grandma?'

She looks at me, but there's no surprise on her face. I feel anxious, but I know Grandma will give me an answer, at least.

She says, 'Your mum is depressed.'

'Depressed?'

'It started as postnatal depression. Post means *after* and natal means *birth.* It happens sometimes when women have babies, and ever since Fin was born, Flora has struggled to feel really well and happy.'

It's good when a grown-up gives you a straight-forward answer.

'Is it Fin's fault?' I ask.

'It's no one's fault, Ellie. Having a baby is a big deal and it can make the chemicals in your body unbalanced and affect how you think and how you feel.'

'Doesn't she love Fin?' I ask.

As much as my little brother irritates me, I don't want Mum *not* to love him. He *is* part of our family after all.

'Of course she does. Your Mum realises she's not well, which is a big step forward. She needs support and kindness and a bit of time to come through this and we all need to help her.'

I think about my big brother, Eddie, who has long tangled hair, is hopeless at timekeeping and can stink a room out at a moment's notice. I wonder if Mum loves him? And with a little pain in my chest – my heart, I think – I wonder if Mum loves me? And most of all, I wonder if she still loves Dad – even just a little bit?

I'm not sure I want to know the answers to these questions, so I tell Grandma about the letters I found hidden in Eddie's bench.

Grandma says, 'Well, I won't ask why you were snooping, Ellie, but perhaps you should just ask Eddie a straight question.'

I say, 'I'd love to, Grandma. But it's only *you* who gives me straight answers.'

This time, Grandma does look surprised.

We sit on her window seat and gaze at the lighthouse. Suddenly, the red light flashes on and off. Then G – O – D – W – A are flashed, one after the other.

Grandma and I look at one another. I feel really strange.

'So *that's* what he's been doing when he's been working late,' says Grandma. She reaches for the brown envelope and writes down the new letters. 'I love puzzles!' she says, cheerfully.

We look at all the letters: **M, L, I, E, S, U, C, K, G, O, D, W and A.**

And, typical of Grandma, she sees happy, nice words: DOG, SLIDE and GECKO. But I see Gilby-type words: DIES, GUILE, SLICK and CODE.

'Is Eddie doing something wrong, Grandma?' I ask.

Grandma doesn't answer. She looks at me and I can read her thoughts exactly: *Ellie Booton, get a grip! Your brother might be a bit immature, a walking fashion disaster and sometimes a bit whiffy - but he's not a bad person.*

Time will tell. I hope she's right.

SATURDAY - 5

I wake up to the sound of wind rattling my windows and seagulls tap dancing on the roof. I dangle my foot out of bed to see how cold it is. It's FREEZING! Herman wags his tail and gives my foot a wash.

I now have a decision to make. Do I go to Eddie and ask him straight out: *What's going on?*

I feel guilty. Eddie lets me use his laptop and never reads my emails, and here I am – about to admit that Cooper and I have been spying on him. Would Eddie feel that he could go through my stuff, because I went through his? I wouldn't like that at all. This is tricky.

The problem is solved for me. I see Eddie get into his car and drive off. I go downstairs. Mum sits at the table in her dressing gown.

She says, 'Good morning, Ellie.'

But it's not a good morning for Mum. She looks tired and when I look into her eyes I see the sadness she tries to hide.

Except it's not a secret any more.

I say, 'I haven't spent any pocket money for ages. Let's go to the Box Brownie. I'll buy you a lovely cup of coffee.'

Mum stares ahead. I'm not sure she's heard me, so I put my arm round her and say, 'I can afford toast as well.' I hug her and kiss her cheek. I say, 'You'll be all right, Mum. You'll get better.'

Even though she squeezes her eyes tight-shut, sadness spills out of them and splashes on the table. I get a paper towel and dry her face.

'You just need a bit of time and lots of kindness and understanding,' I tell her. Mum has always been there for me. I can be there for her. 'A cup of coffee will perk you up and the fresh air will do you lots of good.'

She swallows hard and says, 'It will, Ellie. I'll get dressed.' Her voice is a bit broken. She kisses me and says, 'My darling girl.'

There's no doubt at all. My mum loves me.

I wait for Mum to get ready. My thoughts are a jumbled mess. There's so much to do:-

Help Mum feel better. Keep Elsie safe. Be a friend to Juna. Solve the lighthouse code. Keep an eye on Gilby. Keep track of the countdown posters. Support Miss Askew.

When there are so many things to think about, how do you order your thoughts? How do you decide what's vital and what's not?

For some reason, I think of Cooper and what he said. I go to the whiteboard and I write:

FAMILIARITY BREEDS CONTEMPT

This will help me to focus. I want to WAKE UP and *notice* what's going on! I stand back and study the board and when I turn round, Dad is in the doorway studying *me*.

Dad says, 'Do you know what it means?'

'Of course I do,' I say (thanks to Cooper). 'It means that when you see something *every* day, you stop noticing it.'

Oh, I think. I look at Dad. I've just realised something *very important!*

I say, 'And sometimes, when you see *someone* every day, you *stop noticing them*.'

I eyeball Dad. He blinks and looks at me over his glasses.

'Are we talking about anyone in particular, Ellie?' he asks.

It's time for some straight talking.

I say, 'Mum's depressed. She needs kindness and support. I don't think you see that.'

And this is a FIRST. My clever dad, who is full of opinions because he *thinks,* and writes about what he *thinks* and *thinks* about what he writes – doesn't know what to say.

'She needs us to help her get better,' I tell him.

Dad takes his glasses off and rubs his eyes. OH GOODNESS. I'VE JUST NOTICED SOMETHING ELSE.

I say, 'You're depressed too, Dad.'

Dad says, 'Oh,' puts his glasses on and sort of stumbles out of the kitchen.

Is that *all* he can say?

But a minute later, he reappears and says, 'Very insightful, Ellie. Thank you.'

Mum comes down the stairs carrying Fin. She passes Dad without looking at him. They both look very sad. For a moment, I think Dad might cry.

I say quickly, 'I'm taking Mum to the Box Brownie for coffee. Please come with us, Dad.'

I'm hoping I have enough money for two coffees and all the extras.

To his credit, Dad doesn't hesitate. He says, 'I'd love to, Ellie. Thank you.'

So, for the first time in – I don't know how long – Mum, Dad, Fin and I, go out of the house together.

When we get to the Box Brownie café, Dad wants to pay – but I don't want him to. This was my idea. I want my parents to sit down and talk nicely to one another – and when I tell them this, they *both* look like they're going to cry. *Jeepers!* They look at one another and smile. By the time Cadence brings the coffee over, they're holding hands. I feel VERY RELIEVED. It's almost enough to make me forget about Gilby Flynn – but not quite, because I see him walking towards the café with his minions. He stops to look at a poster tied to a lamp post, tears it down, crumples it up and drop-kicks it onto the beach. Litter bug!

That reminds me – it's day five of the countdown. I wonder what the letter is?

When Gilby reaches the café, he leans against the glass door and peers in. I glance across at Elsie who has spotted him outside. I see Gilby point to his eyes with two fingers, then stab his finger at Elsie. Elsie is suddenly very pale. I think I might be too. Mum and Dad are actually chatting nicely and I really don't want to interrupt them. Cadence is busy steaming milk and looks like she's steaming mad as well. I wonder if Elsie told her we saw Maggie Bell laughing her head off in Jem's van?

That knotty feeling in my stomach is back. Gilby and his minions drift away. It's like they have no purpose at all, other than upsetting people.

Mum and Dad hatch a plan to go to town for lunch by themselves, if Grandma can look after Fin. It's a good idea for them to spend time together. We go out of the café and I run onto the beach, pick up the crumpled poster and put it in my pocket.

When we get home, Grandma tells my parents to go and have a good time. 'Relax,' she says. 'Don't hurry back.'

I go up to my bedroom and smooth out the crumpled poster. It says:

$$5$$
$$C$$

So now there's:

$$10 - 9 - 8 - 7 - 6 - 5$$
$$T - H - E - F - A - C$$

I can't relax though. There's still $4 - 3 - 2 - 1 - 0$, before I find out what the message is.

Mum and Dad drive off. Grandma asks Fin if he'd like to do some baking – and he does, of course, because he likes to get sticky. I ask Grandma if it's OK to take Herman out for a walk.

Grandma says, 'Why don't you meet Elsie and go together?'

I need some company, but I need to be around someone I can be honest with and Elsie isn't that person right now. She's fallen into the trap of hiding things. I don't blame her. It's an easy trap to fall into.

I call Herman and hear him scrabble his paws in the workshop where he's probably been sniffing for spiders. I open the door and let him out. Eddie's upstairs and Grandma is in the pantry with Fin getting the ingredients they need to bake chocolate brownies.

Snap decision. I go into the workshop, head over to Eddie's bench, open the drawer and take out the lighthouse key from the tin. I slip it into my pocket. Herman watches me. I make it back to the kitchen, just as Grandma comes out of the pantry. I pull my face into an expression of pure *innocence*. Herman knows the truth though, and frowns at me with disapproval.

Grandma says, 'Where are you going?'

I say casually, 'On the beach,' which is true. I don't add that I intend to check out the lighthouse as well.

'With Elsie?' asks Grandma.

'Hmm,' I say, instead of yes or no.

DECEPTION – it's a pretty *awful* thing. I don't think I've got what it takes to be good at it.

Herman and I head down the hill. Herman walks nicely on his lead to show me he's a good dog. He looks at me as if to say: *I thought you were good too, Ellie, but I may have been mistaken.*

I reach the Box Brownie and try to sneak past but Elsie sees me and hurries to the door.

She says, 'Wait. I'll come with you.'

Oh dear. She goes inside to get her coat - and then, at the far end of the promenade, I see Cooper. I recognise his walk. He's with a girl – I'm not sure who. *Please* don't let it be Abigail Jennings, I think.

I really need to talk to Cooper about the lighthouse letters. I check the key is still in my pocket. I think: *What if Eddie checks the tin and sees the key is missing?*

One of Dad's sayings is: *Don't panic,* because he thinks people can stay calm in every situation. But he's WRONG. Panic is *real*, and when it happens, you've no choice in the matter. I want to run home and put the key back, but my legs are wobbly. What should I do? My heart starts to thump like a caged kangaroo.

Cooper and the girl walk towards me. Her body language is familiar. I glimpse her bag – khaki with a white skull and crossbones. He's with Juna. I gulp some air and try to calm down.

THINK! *What's going on here? The lighthouse key is in my pocket. I haven't exactly stolen it – but I feel pretty sneaky. I don't like hiding things.*

Cooper and Juna walk up to me.

Cooper says, 'I was heading over to see you when I bumped into Juna.' His look says: *Sorry, she just tagged along.*

It's good to see Cooper, but how can I talk to him with Elsie and Juna there?

Juna looks tired and sad and scared. She might as well have the word, OUTSIDER, stamped on her forehead.

Herman sees this and makes a big fuss of her. Unhappiness worries him. He stares at her with a big grin on his chops. He stamps his feet and wags his tail, as if to say: *I'm glad you're here.*

Juna pats his head nervously, but he's so pleased, it makes her smile.

I say, 'Herman likes you.'

Then Elsie steps out of the café. Herman can't believe his luck. All these people to play with! He wags his tail so hard he nearly falls over. Herman is always open. He never hides.

But, *the rest of us do.*

Eddie hides the lighthouse letters. Juna hides everything, even how lonely she is. Elsie hides her bruise. Cooper would rather freeze to death than tell his dad that his coat was stolen. And Gilby... he hides by the school gates to ambush kids and he only bullies when he thinks no grown-up is watching.

HIDING seems to be the **PROBLEM.**

HIDING isn't good.

Another snap decision...

I let Herman off his lead and he charges down the slipway onto the beach and starts running up the cove, towards the lighthouse. I chase after him.

'Come on,' I yell. 'I've got something to show you.'

When you run against the wind, it's useless trying to talk because it snatches the words out of your mouth and tosses them so high in the air, no one can hear.

Juna can run the fastest, but she measures her pace so we can keep up. Elsie, Cooper and I run shoulder to shoulder – as hard as we can on Juna's heels. Herman barks and leads his pack. The sand is soft and makes running hard, but we don't give up. The sky is blue and clear. The air is cold and salty. Waves thump down on the beach and speed towards us, then drag the pebbles back into the sea. My legs feel like they're going to drop off and I start to laugh. We reach the edge of the cove, panting for breath and drop down in the sand. We *really* need to get into training - you never know when you might need a burst of speed.

'So, what is it you're going to show us?' gasps Elsie.

There's a lot to explain.

I tell Juna about the red letters flashed from the lighthouse and how I thought it must have something to do with Gilby.

Juna nods. 'I think I saw some,' she says.

Elsie tells Juna about the piece of fabric we found on the gatepost and how it's just like Eddie's work-shirt.

Cooper looks at me. I know what he's thinking: *Is it OK to share the story about Eddie?*

I nod.

So Cooper tells Juna how he ran across the field one night and saw Eddie going into the lighthouse. Then I tell everyone about the cut-out letters I found under Eddie's workbench, and all the letters I've seen so far.

All the evidence points to Eddie. My big brother. Who stinks.

I say, 'I thought something bad was going on – but it *can't* be bad. Eddie's not a bad person.'

Everyone agrees, even Juna, who has never even met him. I'm relieved.

The run has made our faces glow. Juna looks different, somehow. Her eyes are brighter. She puts her arm round Herman and he gives her a lick. She laughs. Cooper looks warm in his jacket. He unzips it, closes his eyes and raises his face to the winter sun. His breathing is easy and he doesn't cough. Elsie's hair is caught by the wind. Her bruise is fading though I feel a stab inside when I think of Gilby.

I pull the lighthouse key from my pocket. Cooper takes it and reads the paper tag.

Everyone looks at me. I feel GUILTY.

'It's from Eddie's drawer,' I say.

I know what Cooper's thinking. I answer him, but not out loud. *No, Eddie doesn't know that I've taken it.*

Cooper looks surprised. It's handy that I can read his thoughts, but it's a nuisance that he can read mine.

He stands up.

'Let's go and see what we can find,' he says.

We scramble over the rocks and pull ourselves onto the grass. There's no one about. The gate creaks when we go through. We climb the stone steps and Cooper unlocks the door. It's very heavy - we have to push it hard - but it opens. We step in and the howl of the wind is left behind.

Lighthouses have stone floors and round walls and every sound makes an echo. They are definitely *spooky* places. Climbing the circular steps is pretty scary, because you can't see what's round the corner. Herman doesn't care, so he goes first, then Cooper, then me, then Elsie, then Juna. Herman's not worried though – so there's no one here but us. We go up and up and suddenly we're in a round room and there's light.

The window looks directly towards the Box Brownie café along the promenade. There's a spotlight with a red bulb pointing towards the window, and in front of it is an easel. Stacked neatly to one side there's a pile of tiles, each a cut-out letter.

Cooper says, 'I'll tell you what we've got here. Can you remember them, Ellie?'

'Sure,' I say.

So Cooper goes through the tiles, one by one.

C, L, U, E, K, I, S, M.

Then he takes out **W, A, G, O, D,** from a black bag.

'Those are the letters I found in the workshop,' I say.

'Wait a minute,' says Cooper.

He goes over to the far side of the room. There are three more tiles stacked on a little wooden chair. Cooper shifts them so we can see each one. One tile is I, one tile is U and the third tile has a heart shape cut out of it.

'I love you,' he says.

I feel *awkward*. Cooper goes red.

'Is that part of the code?' I ask.

Suddenly, Herman pricks up his ears. Out of the window we see a green van bouncing across the track towards the lighthouse.

'It's Jem!' Cooper shouts. 'We've got to get out of here!'

We run down the steps like there's no tomorrow. Herman reaches the bottom first. I clip his lead on.

I say, 'Herman. No! You *must not* bark.'

Herman frowns and pins his ears back. He's worried. Why shouldn't he greet Jem? Jem is a friend.

Juna and Elsie run down the steps. Cooper and I struggle to pull the door closed. The key is still in the lock – but there's no time – we have to leave it.

We disappear round the lighthouse just as Jem drives through the gate.

Herman sniffs the air. He wags his tail furiously and starts to pull on his lead.

'Sit!' I command him.

I peep round. Jem and *Eddie* get out of the van. No wonder Herman can smell someone he knows! Jem bounds up the steps to the door.

'It's here!' cries Jem. 'You left it in the lock, you dozy idiot.'

'I took the key home, I swear,' says Eddie.

'Of course you did. That's why it's here. Your brain's turned to mush. It must be love,' says Jem.

They laugh and disappear into the lighthouse.

Herman stays quiet. He's such a good dog. We're hiding, but this is a different sort of hiding - it's fun and exciting. We huddle together against the wind. Ten minutes later, Jem and Eddie come out. Eddie locks the door and makes a big show of putting the key in his pocket. We wait until the van disappears down the track and out of sight.

SUNDAY - 4

Grandma is getting ready to go to church. She fastens her hat on her head with a hatpin and I close my eyes until she's done. I love hats, but I will *never* use a hatpin. NEVER, *ever*. It's asking for trouble.

I say, 'Are you going to find peace, Grandma?'

Grandma says, 'I've got a special favour to ask, and church is the best place to ask it.'

What sort of favour? I wonder.

Grandma reads the question on my face.

She says, 'We don't need much in life to be happy, Ellie. Food to eat, a place that's warm and safe to sleep, the kindness and understanding of others to keep us sane. But if one of those things is missing, life hurts. And when life hurts, sometimes folk bury their feelings so deep they become lost and the hurt carries on.'

'Who are you talking about, Grandma?' I ask.

'Nobody,' says Grandma, 'and everybody. I'm going to say a little prayer and pour it into the River of Good Ideas and Happy Thoughts, and maybe it will wash over those that need it.'

'Will that help?' I ask. I don't quite get the idea of prayer.

'I sure hope so,' says Grandma.

I suddenly wonder if Miss Askew has been hurt. I ask Grandma.

'Most folk have been hurt in one way or another, Ellie,' says Grandma. 'I know of one *huge* hurt in Miss Askew's life. When she was a girl, her little brother was killed in an accident.'

'Oh,' I say. I didn't expect that.

Grandma goes off to church. Dad comes into the kitchen with Fin.

'People are coming for a meeting. Occupy Fin for half an hour,' says Dad.

Take note: he doesn't ask: *Will you* – and he doesn't say: *Please.*

'Who's coming?' I ask.

Dad taps his nose meaning, *mind your own business,* which is very IRRITATING. I wish Dad would answer questions the way Grandma does.

I don't suppose I have a choice. I take Fin into the den. He sits down at his drum kit and starts to play, if you can call it that. BANG-BANG-CRASH. BANG-BANG-CRASH.

I look out of the window and see Jem's van coming up the hill. Then Jem *and* Maggie Bell get out of the van and come into the house. There she goes again, laughing her head off, as usual.

Of all the cheek – Jem coming into *my* house with his new girlfriend. I thought Jem might make a really nice stepdad for Elsie, but I was wrong.

Eddie puts his head round the door and says, 'Fin, play

with something a bit quieter, will you?'

'No,' says Fin, and bangs his drum harder.

Eddie gives me a pleading look and shuts the door.

Then Susannah arrives on her moped. I hear her say, 'Hello fellow conspirators.'

They all say, 'Hello Susannah.'

Susannah says, 'What are these little posters? They're plastered everywhere. 4-E. What's that all about?'

'No idea,' says Eddie.

'They're different every day,' says Maggie.

'Curious,' says Jem.

'Very curious,' says Dad.

None of them are as smart as Cooper who worked out straight away that it was a countdown.

4E? That means the message so far is: **THE FACE**.

They all troop up to Dad's office.

Fin sings along to his drums. It's not a good sound. I think he might be as musical as me, poor thing.

Have you ever noticed that when someone tells you to *mind your own business*, or words to that effect, it makes you determined to find out what's going on? *Fellow conspirators?* What does that mean?

I say to Fin, 'Do you want to play a very special game?'

Fin nods.

'We have to be very quiet, like little mice,' I whisper.

'Why?' asks Fin.

'It's a secret. We have to go upstairs and not make a sound, and then come back down again very, very quietly.'

Fin is quite pleased with the idea. Oh no! I *am* a spy - and

I'm teaching Fin how to be SNEAKY. He's easily led, like Eddie. I think I will worry about him when he gets older. We creep up the stairs. Herman tags on. We tiptoe up to Dad's office door.

I whisper, 'Shh, quiet as a mouse.'

I press my ear to the door…

I hear Dad say, 'So, Operation Lighthouse… Is everything ready?'

'All the letters are cut and the equipment's checked,' says Eddie. 'We tested the letters at night. You can see them clearly from the Box Brownie. So, all systems are go!'

'So long as you don't lose the lighthouse key again, we'll be just fine,' says Jem.

'Oh, for goodness sake, Eddie,' groans Dad.

'I don't know how it happened,' says Eddie, sounding a bit stressed.

'You're tired, Eddie,' says Susannah kindly. 'You've put a lot of work into this project.'

'It wasn't really lost,' says Jem. 'He'd just left it in the keyhole.'

'*Good grief!*' cries Dad. 'We promised to keep the lighthouse secure. I might as well have put Herman in charge of security!'

There's a silence. It's a bit uncomfortable, though Herman looks pleased and wags his tail.

'I wish she'd let us do more,' says Susannah, changing the subject.

'She has such a problem showing her feelings,' says Maggie.

'We just have to respect that and keep it simple. At least she's finally agreed to a get-together to celebrate the end of the play,' says Susannah.

Oh I see. *She* is Miss Askew.

'And has Cadence agreed to host it at the Box Brownie?' asks Dad.

'It's all sorted,' says Jem. 'It's a relief to tell her what's going on. All these secret meetings. She thought I'd copped off with Maggie behind her back.'

Maggie laughs her head off. 'Sorry, Jem,' she says. 'You're not my type.'

Everyone laughs for some reason.

Dad says, 'Operation Lighthouse *has* to be secret. The cat must stay firmly in the bag, especially with kids like Ellie and Elsie around.'

Everyone laughs some more. My mouth drops open. *WHAT A CHEEK!*

Maggie says, 'If they knew what was going on, they'd spill the beans for sure. They need protecting for their own good.'

I nearly choke. *PUR-LEASE!* We're protecting the grown-ups, *NOT* the other way around!

'If they knew Miss Askew was going to Rwanda, they'd want to make a big deal of everything. It has to be minimal. Good luck is all she can cope with,' says Dad.

Excuse me! I already know Miss Askew is going to Rwanda and I haven't said a word to anyone. I hear a chair move.

'Anyone for coffee?' asks Susannah.

I grab Fin's hand and we hurry downstairs and back into the den. I pick up a dictionary from the bookcase and look up the word MINIMAL.

Minimal: very small indeed.

So now it's easy to guess that Miss Askew has agreed to go to a *minimal* party at the Box Brownie café, which is the perfect place to see a message flashed from the lighthouse.

Twenty minutes later, they all stampede downstairs. Jem and laugh-a-lot Maggie go off together, Dad goes back to his office and Eddie and Susannah disappear into the kitchen.

Fin and I creep up to my room. He's not normally allowed in here because he's sticky and he picks things up and makes a mess. He's very pleased and cuddles my old teddy. I look at my little brother. I wonder how I would feel if he had an accident and died? I get a lump in my throat.

How do people live their lives when their hearts have been broken? Perhaps like Miss Askew – who keeps busy and helps others and locks her private feelings deep inside. I think I understand Miss Askew a bit better now. Do hearts mend, I wonder?

I pick Fin up and give him a big hug.

I say, 'I love you, little Fin.'

And Fin says, 'I love you too, Melly Moo,' and then he adds, 'even though you stink of poo.' He laughs and laughs.

My sticky brother is annoying. Still, I'm surprised and a bit ashamed that this is the first time I've ever told him that I love him. I don't think I realised it before today.

The lighthouse letters are written down in my notebook. I open it and read them.

M, L, I, E, S, U, C, K, G, O, D, W, A.

What did Dad say? *It has to be minimal. Good luck is all she can cope with.*

Wait a minute…*Good luck Miss Askew?*

From the letters I can make: GOD LUCK, and then: MIS AEW.

And then – of course – I think of how Eddie will flash the letters. He will put each letter on the easel in front of the spotlight. So for GOOD, he will flash the 'O' twice, flash L-U-C-K, then M-I and flash the S twice, then A, then reuse the S and the K, then flash E and W.

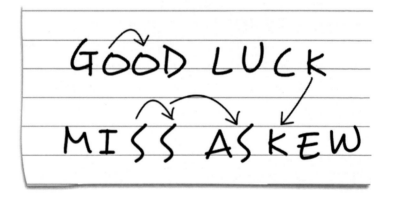

I don't believe it. I've cracked the lighthouse code!

GOOD GRIEF! What a let-down! There's not even a *thank you* in there: for *all* her HARD WORK; for *all* her CARE; for *all* the TIME she has put into producing every play that has ever been performed at the school (well, almost).

I feel really… disappointed.

Afternoon rehearsal

I walk up the hill with Elsie and we meet Juna and Cooper at the top of Curly Lane. I have the latest poster in my hand.

'Today's letter is **E**,' I say, 'so the message is: **THE FACE.**'

'THE FACE of what though?' asks Elsie.

'Or who?' says Cooper.

'We'll know on Thursday, which is the first performance of the play,' I say, feeling stressed.

Juna shrugs.

'Don't you think it's odd?' I ask her.

But Juna, as usual, prefers to say nothing.

It's strange walking to school on a Sunday. It doesn't feel right somehow. To be honest, *nothing* feels right. I'm wondering if I should tell them about Miss Askew's party (if you can call it that) and the feeble message these uninspired grown-ups plan to flash from the lighthouse.

We're just going through the school gates when we see a black BMW slow down and park on the zigzag lines (which is, technically, not allowed).

Gilby slithers out and the car slides away. He keeps his head down and hurries past us, which is very unusual. He normally has lots to say, but his minions aren't there to provide an audience for him today.

We make our way to the school hall and everyone goes their separate ways. Cooper heads into the wings, ready to shift scenery. Juna joins the waifs and strays at the far side of the stage. Elsie stands centre stage looking pretty lonely, and I join Miss Askew.

'Hello Ellie,' she says sadly.

She looks extra-beige today – like there's no colour in her life at all. She tears out a piece of paper from her notebook and hands it to me. It's a list of things-to-do, marked DA for Dorothy Askew and EB for Ellie Booton.

THINGS TO DO!

* DA to email press release to local newspaper, the Peregrine Post (DONE)
* DA to remind everyone to eat fresh fruit
− NO ONE must catch a cold!
* DA to remind everyone to wear a watch
− NO ONE must be late!
* DA and EB to pick up photocopied programmes from reprographics (TODAY!)
* EB to distribute rehearsal and performance times to cast and stagehands (TODAY!)
* DA to thank cast and stagehands for all their hard work − (remember token gifts for everyone)

The paper is imprinted with another message, probably

written on the sheet above it. I just can't help myself. I hold the paper up to the light. I make out: *Special pressie for Ellie for keeping me sane.*

I get a lump in my throat. I swallow and look over at Miss Askew. She glances at me and says, 'No turning back now, Ellie. I'm committed – no matter what.'

I wonder if she's talking about the play or going to Rwanda? I say, 'Everything will work out.'

'You're a glass half-full, Ellie Booton,' says Miss Askew and smiles.

This is nice to hear because, for a while, I've been a glass half-empty.

Rehearsal isn't a *complete* disaster. Elsie's singing just gets better. The waifs and strays get their act together and give it a lot of wellie (as Eddie would say) and Gilby behaves and shows a bit of talent. He has a good singing voice. It's a shame – no – it's *tragic* - that his speaking voice spills out so many ugly thoughts. He's completely WASTING his life making enemies. If he could just concentrate on the good side of his personality, (does he have one, I wonder?) he might not be such an EVIL TOAD – though that's unfair, because toads aren't evil.

I meet up with Cooper, Juna and Elsie after rehearsal and we walk down the hill together. We're all quiet, especially Juna. Only the skull and crossbones on her bag signal how unhappy she is.

At the top of Curly Lane, Cooper and Juna head off towards their homes on the other side of town. Cooper turns round and calls, 'See you tomorrow,' but Juna doesn't look back. She shifts the bag on her shoulder and a piece of paper flutters to the ground. Elsie runs and picks it up – but she doesn't bother to call Juna back.

'It's nothing,' she says, handing me a scrap of paper with one of Juna's strange doodled faces on it.

I feel – *anxious*. The lighthouse code has been solved – so why do I feel that something *terrible* is about to happen?

MONDAY - 3

My mum is depressed and she finds it hard to get out of bed every morning, or to comb her hair, or choose nice clothes to wear. When she smiles, it often doesn't reach her eyes, if you know what I mean. She hardly ever cries, but sometimes I think she might be crying on the inside. I've known this for a while, but I'm just starting to understand it.

I go downstairs to get my breakfast.

Grandma sits at the table staring at Dad's scribble on the whiteboard.

A FAMILY IS MUSIC. FOR HARMONY, STAY IN TUNE!

'What's that about, Grandma?' I ask. I mean, Dad's singing is legendary, but not in a good way. He can start a stampede just by singing Happy Birthday. I don't know *how* he got chosen to write about the Watford Warbler.

Grandma says, 'Walter's finally realised he has to sing from the same hymn sheet as the rest of us -'

'We have to sing hymns now?' I don't like the sound of that.

'- and stay in tune with Flora,' adds Grandma.

Still not sure what you're saying, Grandma.

Grandma listens to my thoughts.

She sighs and says, 'Walter needs to understand Flora much better than he does. Reading a face, or what's going on in someone's head is a real skill. It's like cracking a code, Ellie. Communication is *much* more than words and people thrive when they feel understood. That's what's been lacking. *Understanding.*'

Oh, I see. Well, no one seems to know what's going on in *my* head. Grandma talks about the River of Good Ideas and Happy Thoughts but *my* thoughts are being tossed about on the Rough Sea of Worry.

I set off to school. My eyes hurt. I have a headache. Elsie isn't at the café, so I walk along the promenade alone. There are new posters tied up with green stripy string. I rip one down from a lamp post. Today it says:

I stuff it in my pocket. Cooper is waiting at the corner of Curly Lane. I'm glad to see him, but I can't smile.

'You OK?' he asks.

'Never better,' I say, flatly.

He puts his arm round me and gives me a squeeze.

'Spill the beans,' he says.

I take a deep breath. 'I've cracked the lighthouse code.'

'Yeah,' he says. 'Me too.'

I stop in my tracks. 'You have?'

'Once I saw the letters for ASKEW,' he says, 'the rest

was obvious.'

When I first met Cooper, I thought he was just another silly boy. But he's not.

'You're smart,' I say.

'Don't sound so shocked,' says Cooper, but he smiles and looks at his feet. We walk on. I don't want to tell him that I only managed to work it out by sneaking around and listening through doors.

Then Cooper stops. He turns and looks at me.

He says, 'I love you.'

'*What?*' I say.

'The other message,' says Cooper quickly. 'I *heart* U. No one would send Miss Askew that message.'

Oh. I'd forgotten about that. I can't imagine that's meant for Miss Askew either. I wonder if anyone loves her at all.

The morning is *l-o-n-g* and *p-a-i-n-f-u-l*. If you've ever had a headache you'll know that it's almost impossible to be interested in anything. I wish I could just go home. And if I had another wish, it would be to survive the play and for it to be over. Then it will be Christmas. I will stay in my bedroom and read books, and take Herman for walks on the beach. And I won't think about Elsie or Juna, or the lighthouse, or posters, or Miss Askew, or Gilby, or my poor mum who struggles to be happy.

But that's impossible. I *can't not* think about Mum – which is a DOUBLE NEGATIVE, because I *always* find myself thinking about her. I just want her to get better.

Oh, my head hurts.

Juna roams around the playground by herself. She could hang out with me and Elsie, but I suppose some habits are hard to break. It's a good idea to have a group of friends. Real friends – not like the load of silly friends that Abigail Jennings has, who spend so much time posing, they forget who they actually are. They're mean to everyone, even each other – and when they laugh, they're laughing *at* someone – like Elsie in rehearsal – though Elsie probably has the best voice in the whole school – and she's probably one of the prettiest girls too. How can people *not* like Elsie?

Elsie and I cross the playground to the running track. We've started to sprint at lunch time because it's good to be able to turn on a bit of speed. I see Juna. She sits, huddled on some steps, doodling something - head down, closed off from the world as usual.

Elsie goes on the track and runs, but I can't. With every step, my head goes thud, thud, THUD. I have a sore throat too. I *can't* get sick. I can't let Miss Askew down.

I walk over to Juna and sit down. She glances up, but keeps drawing - and for some reason, I start to cry.

I know, I know. BIG BABY stuff.

I'm not the sort of girl who just blubs for no reason. It's annoying and *very embarrassing*.

Juna looks up, surprised. 'What's wrong, Ellie?' she asks.

'I don't feel well.'

'You look awful,' she says.

That cheers me up no end.

She stands up and says, 'I'll get Elsie.'

I reach out and take her hand. I don't want any fuss.

Quietness. Stillness. That's what I need.

'No, Juna,' I say. 'Please stay with me.'

Juna's eyes focus on me, like she's seeing me for the *first* time. She has kind eyes. She sits down, puts her arm round me and whispers, 'I'm here.'

Thunder clouds are on the horizon, but there's a sudden burst of light. I rest my head on her shoulder and close my eyes. The noise of the playground fades. Rays of winter sun splash my face with heat. Behind my eyes, I see an orange glow which seems to slowly sink into my bones. I'm a tiny speck floating on a vast orange sea. The calm before the storm.

I wake up on the sofa in the den. Fin is two inches away from my nose, his eyes like saucers staring into mine. He's sticky and snotty and I think he's dribbled on me.

He coughs in my face and says, 'Want to play?'

Herman pushes in, sticks his nose in my ear, has a good sniff, then licks my cheek. No wonder I'm sick, I think. Mum comes into the den.

She says, 'Poor girl. You're not well.'

Grown-ups are so good at stating the obvious.

'What happened?' I ask.

Mum explains that I fell asleep on Juna's shoulder, so Elsie went to get a teacher, who thought I might have a high temperature and called Mum. I think I might have been sick on someone's shoes – so I'm not keen to hear too much detail.

'I'm sorry, Mum,' I say. 'I don't want to make you

unhappy.'

'Don't be silly,' says Mum. 'You light up my life. You are the colour orange, Ellie.'

'That's funny,' I say, 'I dreamed I was orange.'

Mum smiles with her eyes and helps me to sit up. She wipes my face with a damp cloth and gives me a glass of water to sip.

'I can't be ill, Mum,' I say. 'Miss Askew needs me.'

'Well, she'll have to do without you – for forty-eight hours, at least,' says Mum.

That's the rule. If you throw up, you have to stay off school for at least two days. Mum hugs me. I notice her hair smells peachy. Fin hands me Bob the Builder, his favourite toy and gives me a snotty kiss. I feel loved, but I just need to be quiet. There's no such thing as peace though. Suddenly, I'm a star attraction.

Dad comes into the den. He peers at me over his glasses, puts his hand on my forehead and says, 'Deary me. What have you been up to, kid?'

Nanna and Gramps come in to inspect me. Nanna tells me I must eat. 'You must feed a cold and starve a fever,' she says.

'She has a fever,' says Gramps.

'She has a cold,' says Nanna.

Then Eddie pokes his head round the door and says, 'You puked on Juna.'

Oh no. That's too much information.

'Don't suppose you fancy a nice hot curry?' says Eddie, and laughs.

UGH! At the moment, I don't want to imagine that curry exists in the entire universe.

'Go away you big ape,' I say.

Then Mum brings me my soft pillow and a jug of chilled water with lemon and honey.

She says softly, 'Is there anything I can get for you, Ellie?'

But I don't want anything. Just to be left alone. They all go off to eat in the kitchen and I stay in the den, cosy on the sofa.

I put my glass on the coffee table. There's a scrap of paper with something written on it. I pick it up. It says:

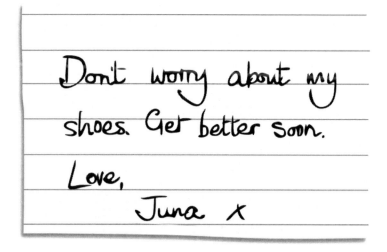

Don't worry about my shoes. Get better soon. Love, Juna x

I turn the scrap of paper over. There are two more of her strange doodled faces.

Juna has eyes that aren't green, or brown, or blue. They're grey, like the seals I sometimes see on the beach. What was it that Grandma said? *Reading a face is like cracking a code.*

Oh boy... I don't feel good... If you have a high temperature, it can make your brain go a bit wonky.

How is it that I suddenly **KNOW** what tomorrow's poster will be without even seeing it? **I KNOW** what Wednesday's poster will be as well. I also **KNOW** who's putting them up. I might even know why.

This is a really BIG WORRY.

I hear the wind trying to slice the house in half and the rain smashing against the window. It's going to be a very stormy night…

TUESDAY - 2

darkness - someone hovering

leave me alone – please

am I awake? am I -

- a ship on waves so high I might never see sky again - cold, black water - flashing light - on - off - howling and crashing - terrible noise! - am I broken? - falling - grab hold! - whatever happens, I mustn't let go - help me - the door is so heavy - push - push - tumble in - sucked down - shouldn't steps go up? - who's there? - do I know you? - be still - quiet as a mouse - don't breathe - don't breathe - don't breathe . . . MUST breathe - a skull? - so glad to see you - NO! DON'T GO! - sliding shape - dead eyes of a shark - DON'T PUSH ME! NOOO!

FALLING! -

up and up and up and up and up and up...

air... breathing... light...

The storm has blown itself out. It's bright and still. Mum

pops her head round the door. We both look at Dad who's curled up on my window seat under a blanket, fast asleep with his mouth wide open.

'He looks like a Venus fly trap,' I say.

She brings in a tray of tea for them and a glass of water for me, and wakes Dad up by tickling his ear with a seagull feather from my desk.

'Good grief... My back's *killing* me!' mutters Dad, making a big fuss of swinging his legs to the floor and trying to sit up. Not a pretty sight. 'Have I been hit by a tram?'

'Deary me,' laughs Mum. She seems quite amused seeing Dad in pain. She takes his hands and pulls him into a sitting position, ignoring his loud groans. I watch. If I keep my head still and don't make any sudden moves – well – it's bearable.

'You're stiff because you never leave your office,' she says. 'You're an old man.'

'Right,' says Dad, 'today, I'm starting over. I mean it! I'm going for a walk on the beach -'

'Get the flags out,' says Mum.

'- and you're coming with me.'

Dad smacks Mum on the bottom. Goodness – she laughs again! Hang on a minute... This is all very nice – seeing my parents have a giggle for a change – but what about me?

Dad tells me that he stayed with me through the night because I was delirious – which means that my temperature was so high I was seeing pink elephants. How does he know, I wonder? I can't remember elephants, but I have a vague memory of sharks.

I need to go to school and talk to someone about my

REALLY BIG WORRY – but if I tried to get up this morning, I'd fall over. So – *forget it,* Ellie Booton – it's just not going to happen.

Dad seems to know what I'm thinking.

He says, 'Don't worry about school, Ellie. You need to get better. The world will keep turning whether you're there or not.'

It's not like Dad to be sensitive. Maybe he really is trying to tune in.

Mum chips in, 'And with a bit of luck, you might be well enough for school on Friday.'

FRIDAY?! That's going to be **ONE DAY TOO LATE!** There's someone I *must* see before day zero.

Oh, in case you were wondering… the poster today (even though I haven't seen it and no one has told me) is:

2
F

and tomorrow's poster will be:

1
A

So the countdown message is:

THE FACE OF A…

Wednesday's child is full of woe

Morning...

I was born on a Wednesday. According to a rhyme,* this makes me full of woe - which basically means that I'm a glass half-empty kinda kid.

I'm sorry if I've given this impression. I was getting ill – and worry doesn't do anyone any good – and it certainly doesn't change anything, that's for sure. I just want to get back to being a glass half-full kid, as soon as possible.

The rhyme's not true, either. Eddie was born on a Tuesday (*Tuesday's child is full of grace*). Excuse me. Eddie is *DISgraceful*. And Fin was born on a Saturday (*Saturday's child works hard for a living*). Excuse me again. Fin doesn't even brush his own teeth! Oh dear – I take that back. Eddie can be a *bit* graceful when he's with Susannah – and Fin works hard at being annoying.

I'm not full of woe. I have a plan. I am a model patient. I drink loads and eat fruit, rest, blow my nose and take gulps of fresh air from my open window. And I wait *patiently* because I need to see someone, and it's not going to be easy.

Eddie pops his head round the door. He's in a helpful mood so I make the most of it. I ask if I can chat to

Susannah, so he rings her on his smartphone, gives it to me, then goes to fetch his laptop which I want to borrow. I tell her about my REALLY BIG WORRY and explain my plan. She listens and agrees to help. By the end of the conversation, I feel much more positive. What would I do without Susannah?

When Eddie comes back with his laptop, I Google: ORANGE.

'It's a fruit, you dope. Has your brain been juiced?' says Eddie, rudely.

'Susannah told me about auras,'* I say. 'Mum said I'm orange.'

'That's because you're an orang-utan,' says Eddie.

I ignore him. According to the Internet, orange is a good, helpful colour. It gives people a feeling of warmth and strength and helps them to heal and be optimistic. That's good to know. I notice that Mum is wearing a new orange T-shirt today. I think she's definitely trying to find her happy self again. You can't do that if you wear black every day – look what happened to Queen Victoria* – she was sad for a very long time. Black makes people disappear.

Afternoon...

Dad comes in to check me. He takes my temperature and tells me I'm cooked. There's opera wafting from his office, but to tell the truth, I'm almost used to it by now. The Watford Warbler can hold a tune. Anyway, Mum says she likes it – so that's a good reason to have it blaring away –

and Eddie told me that opera makes lima beans grow faster, so it might make Fin sprout up, because when he's bigger he might not be so sticky.

Why am I thinking like this? Maybe Dad's right – my brain *is* cooked.

I ask Dad to get me some paper and pens. I've got time to kill. If Pavarotti discovered he was a great singer by singing, maybe I'll discover I'm a great writer if I write? So Dad gets on his hands and knees and pulls out plastic boxes from beneath the bottom bunk. I give him instructions and he makes a complete mess of following them.

'No, not *that* one!' I say. 'I want the one with the indigo lid… *No,* not that one! That's lilac… *No,* that's lavender. The *indigo* lid, I said.'

'Good grief,' says Dad. 'How many shades of purple can there be?'

Dad finally pulls out the right box of pens. He would make a very poor assistant.

'Get better soon, Ellie. I mean it. Much more of this, and I'll have to go into a rest home to recover,' says Dad.

Hardly. I've only been in bed one day! His knees crack when he stands up.

'Crikey!' he says. 'Your mum's right. I *am* an old man.'

Dad will be fifty on Christmas Eve, so I guess he's pretty ancient.

'Can you close the window, please?' I ask.

Dad sighs. 'And then can I go back to work, madam?'

'When you've closed the window,' I say.

So Dad, being old and not used to doing anything

practical, tries to close the window. It's stiff, so he opens it wider for a moment, just as someone opens the door downstairs, causing a huge draft which sucks the paper off my bed and sends it fluttering into the air.

And then… I have an **IDEA…**

But first, I must talk to someone about my REALLY BIG WORRY.

A picture paints a thousand words

I've spent all afternoon making notes and thinking about my plan. I've managed to eat some dinner because I need the strength to get better as soon as possible.

The rain has finally stopped. It's half past eight and pitch black outside. There's a lot of cold, empty space out there. I hear the sound of Susannah's moped spluttering up the hill.

She comes straight up to my bedroom, even before she goes to see Eddie, and gives me the biggest hug. Her T-shirt says: KEEP CALM & STAY STRONG.

She says, 'All right, Ellie. Let's try to sort this out.'

And this is what happens... Susannah speaks with my parents and Eddie. I'm not sure what she tells them, but five minutes later she's back and she helps me get dressed and we go downstairs. I feel a bit wobbly on my legs. Eddie is waiting in the hall holding his car keys.

Susannah and I get into Eddie's car and he drives to the far end of the promenade. He switches off the engine and we all sit quietly and wait. I start to wonder - *have I got this wrong? Have I misunderstood?* But then, I see someone climb over the fence onto the promenade. I hold my breath. *Am I right?*

Susannah whispers, 'Good luck, Ellie.'

I get out of the car. I don't want to frighten her.

'*Juna,*' I call softly.

Juna twists round and screams. She stands in a pool of light with a poster in one hand and a ball of stripy string in the other.

'It's all right,' I say. 'It's only me.'

Juna and I sit on the floor in front of the fire in the den. Herman sits next to Juna. He looks worried, but he wags his tail anyway. He knew from the moment he met her that she was a good person - but even good people can get it wrong.

Juna is shaken up and so am I. It's frightening to realise that she's roaming about at night and her parents don't even know it. Her mum has a night-time cleaning job and her Dad watches television and drinks beer.

'How did you know it was me?' she asks.

I show her the scrap of paper with her doodles.

'Oh,' says Juna.

'They're clever,' I say. *[Can you see the clues in the faces? There are more of Juna's doodles* at the back of my journal.]*

Juna hugs her knees. There's a silence and it needs to be filled. I have a question to ask.

I say, 'The face of a - *what?*'

I'm pretty sure the answer won't be HERO.

Juna doesn't speak. She reaches into her bag, pulls out a poster and hands it to me. Her hand shakes a little.

It's a pretty good sketch of Gilby Flynn. His face is drawn in a ZERO, and under the zero is another word for BULLY. Ideally, it's not a word you should call people.

I don't blame her – I really don't. Juna is probably the kid he's bullied most and for the longest time. Gilby has made her life a misery. He needs to be named and shamed – but not this way. This could get her into trouble and she doesn't deserve that.

Juna stares at the floor and blinks hard. Then she starts to cry. Tears drip off her chin, onto the carpet.

'It's going to be all right,' I tell her. 'You don't need to put these posters up. We'll tell people about him.'

Juna nods. She's very tired. I read her thoughts – they're misty and grey, the colour of her eyes. Juna doesn't have anyone to tell. No one is interested. That's what she believes, anyway.

How frightening. We all need somebody to turn to. I don't have lots of people – only a few, I suppose – but that's all you need.

I think: *Juna can turn to me. And if she has me, she also has my family.* Thoughts swirl in my head. They're all sorts of colours: peachy shades of orange, splashes of sky blue, hints of lavender, swirls of rose. They're too complicated and colourful to put into words. Anyway, actions speak louder than words. A hug is a good start. I put my arm round her and she rests her head on my shoulder.

There's a gentle tap on the door.

Mum puts her head round and says softly, 'Visitor.'

And in walks Cooper.

Herman is a meeter and greeter, a barker, a bouncer, a tail thrasher – but he's also very sensitive – so he stands quietly and wags his tail, then lies by Juna and rests his head in her lap. He knows she's sad.

Cooper takes in the scene. He doesn't say a thing.

'Don't worry,' I say. 'You won't catch the dreaded lurgy. It's ages since I threw up.'

Cooper smiles. He's not worried about that – of course he isn't. He's worried about the bullying, Elsie – and of course, *Juna*. She's been a shadow for the longest time.

Cooper kneels down and puts his hand on her shoulder. He leans forward, looks deeply into her eyes and says, 'Tell me... How are your shoes?'

We have to laugh.

Then he looks at Juna's shoes, pulls a face and says, 'They're not *the ones*, right?'

So when Mum comes in with chocolate cake, we're all laughing and Herman decides he can wag his tail furiously and take an interest in cake.

Oh – I'll just say – chocolate isn't good for dogs – it's a sort of poison. And before anyone says anything, I eat carrots and broccoli and sensible stuff most of the time – *honestly!* Anyway, laughter plus chocolate equals one of life's richest pleasures, Grandma says – and she's hardly ever wrong.

So – now it's time to tell them about my **IDEA...**

Which is...

*... **a string of bunting to decorate the Box Brownie café for Miss Askew's leaving do... Tra la!***

OK. I can hear you – LOUD and clear! Are you *joking??? PATHETIC!!!*

Hang on. This is what I'm thinking... Mum says, *Get the flags out,* when there's something to celebrate (though granted, she says it sarcastically when Dad needs praising like a little boy). It always makes me think of a string of bunting. I've seen posters flapping in the wind, wet and torn, but still carrying an important message. And when Dad was trying to shut my window and all the paper blew off my bed... these thoughts collided.

I have a box of plastic paper. You can get it wet, crumple it up – and it doesn't get damaged. It can be cut into the shape of a flag. It can be punched and threaded with string.

WHAT IF we all wrote our own message to Miss Askew on pieces of plastic paper, and threaded them together to make bunting? We could hang it around the Box Brownie café and she would be surrounded by good thoughts and love without even knowing it. Then afterwards, she could read them in private. She might cry – but at least she would know *how much* we care for her and she could take all those good thoughts with her to Rwanda.

I explain all of this to Juna and Cooper.

'What do you think?' I ask.

Juna says, 'It's a great idea, Ellie – but how could we organise this? We can't announce it in assembly, can we?'

No. But we *can* tell the people who we **TRUST**. And the people *we* trust, know people *they* trust. There are lots of good people out there – we just have to make the connections. **Bad people and bullies are DEFINITELY in the minority.**

I say, 'One person starts it off with a big pile of paper. They take one piece and they divide the rest of the paper between two trusted friends. Then those friends do the same,

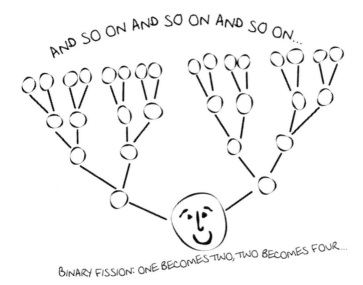

BINARY FISSION: ONE BECOMES TWO, TWO BECOMES FOUR...

149

and they each divide the paper between two other trusted friends - and so on, until all the paper has gone.'

'Binary fission,' says Cooper. 'One becomes two, two becomes four, four becomes eight…'

'Exactly,' I say. 'And all these friends have ONE day to write their message and pass on the paper. And the next day, *all* the messages are handed back.'

'Like a chain,' says Juna.

'If it works, the paper will come back to the person who started it off. Then all we have to do is string the messages together.'

'Utter genius,' says Cooper.

Let me tell you - when you're under the weather and worried and, suddenly, there's chocolate cake and someone saying you're a genius - it can make you feel a *whole* heap better.

We go upstairs to my room. Juna sits on the window seat and looks round. I show Cooper where the box of plastic paper is.

Juna swallows and says, 'Cooper, it was me. I put the posters up.'

'I know,' says Cooper, disappearing under the bunk with Herman belly crawling after him.

Juna and I look at one another, shocked.

Herman must lick Cooper's face, because he goes, 'Eww, Herman!' He drags the box out and wrestles Herman who's found a ball and wants to play.

'*How* do you know?' asks Juna.

Cooper shrugs. 'When we were on the beach you told us

you saw letters flashed from the lighthouse. You would need to be on the promenade at night to see them and that's where the posters start from... I put two and two together.'

He *really* doesn't realise how smart he is.

'Oh,' says Juna.

'What did you have planned for zero?' asks Cooper.

Juna hands him a poster from her bag.

Cooper looks at it and smiles. He doesn't blame her either.

'He deserves it,' says Cooper. 'He's a bully. He stole my coat.'

Another shock. 'Why?' I ask. Gilby is a walking fashion show. The last thing he needs is another boy's jacket.

'I guess he thought it might be fun to watch me freeze.'

'He's so nasty,' I say.

We all sit and think for a few moments. Gilby has pushed and shoved, stolen, threatened, frightened and hurt. How did he get away with it for so long?

Simple. Everyone who has seen Gilby in action and has said nothing, has helped him. We're all responsible.

'You don't need to put the last poster up, Juna,' says Cooper. 'We're in this together. We'll sort this out.'

'Let's get through the play in one piece, then we'll go to Mrs Jago and tell her what's been going on,' I say.

Juna nods.

It will be a relief to tell our stories about Gilby Flynn. Better late than never – though I wish we hadn't gone through this in the first place.

I open the box of plastic paper. Juna looks anxious. I see

her thoughts. They're the shape and colour of rain clouds. Juna doesn't have too many trusted people in her life.

I say, 'You start this off, Juna. Take one piece and pass the rest of the paper to two people you trust.'

I place the paper in front of her. Cooper and I look at her expectantly. Juna, silently and solemnly, takes a piece for herself then divides the paper into two and hands one pile to Cooper and the other to me.

Her eyes are grey, but the sadness has gone.

Thursday's child has far to go...

Body temperature: 38 degrees Celsius (normalish)
Energy levels: Walking: OK. Running: out of the question.
Head: Wuzzy. Don't ask me to explain Pythagoras today.
Outlook: It can only get better.

I'm still a bit wobbly but I'm back at school. It is day ZERO and tonight will be the first performance of the play. Elsie agrees that we must report Gilby, but first, we need to get the play over and done with. All of us have handed paper on to trusted friends. I gave mine to Elsie and Susannah and Cooper gave his to Cody Child and Aaron Hicknell. Then Cody gave his paper to Charlie Myatt and Erin Forster, and Elsie gave hers to Purdy Wallace and Thomas Tregerthen. And Thomas gave his to Michael Farrow and Robbie Parker... and then I lost track. There are LOADS of nice, trustworthy kids in school. It spread outside school as well, because the paper I gave to Susannah went to Maggie Bell and Grandma, and they passed it on to folk who know Miss Askew – some even went to school with her when she was a girl!

So – tomorrow, fingers crossed – it will all come back.

Thursday lunch time: the very LAST rehearsal before the REAL THING

Miss Askew says, 'I'm glad to see you back, Ellie. I've missed your organisational skills.'

She seems a bit stressed, but knowing her as I do, she's trying to keep it together. Her nose is red, like mine. She's got a cold – but she's obviously been taking Night Nurse or something, because there's no way she can call in sick now. We have to see this through to the bitter end.

Miss Askew shouts hoarsely, 'Well done everyone. In the theatre it's considered **BAD LUCK** to wish anyone **GOOD LUCK**. Theatre folk say **BREAK A LEG** instead. But please, for the love of all that is *sacred* – **DO NOT** take this **LITERALLY!**' And then she smiles and says to me: 'It's too soon to say *get the flags out* – but I think we're getting there.'

A couple of boys from Year 7 come into the hall by mistake, shriek and practically fall over one another backing out. I'm distracted and I completely miss what happens next. Everybody does – except Cooper. And this is what he sees…

Elsie walks to the side of the stage to collect her bag. Gilby pushes her into the stage curtain and they disappear from sight.

In this short space of time, Gilby grabs Elsie's ear, twists it, and tells her that he is going to HURT her during the actual play, and there is NOTHING she can do about it.

What I *do* see is Elsie stumbling out of the folds of

curtain looking as white as a sheet. I catch sight of Gilby a few steps ahead. He flashes me an ugly smile. In *s-l-o-w* motion I see Cooper spring like a ninja and swing Gilby round. They stand nose to nose, then Gilby gives Cooper an almighty push and makes a run for it. Cooper falls back and as Gilby tries to jump over him, his foot gets caught on Cooper's arm and Gilby, with a look of utter surprise, goes down like a sack of spuds and he rolls off the stage with a… *CRACK*.

You know when you're in a bit of shock – it's hard to tell a story without sounding a bit FREAKED OUT, so I'll make a list instead:

1. Miss Askew cries out, 'Marvellous - a literal thinker!' which I think is strange, until I think about the definition of 'literal' and what she's just said about breaking a leg - because it's obvious that Gilby has done just that.
2. Gilby is given First Aid and told, very nicely, that everything will be all right.
3. Miss Askew calls an ambulance.
4. Mrs Jago, the head teacher sweeps in, waves her arms around, then goes off to phone Gilby's dad.

Gilby was born on a Thursday, apparently – so this rhyme is true: *Thursday's child has far to go.* It's a long way to the hospital and it will seem even longer with Mrs Jago for company. Gilby's dad opts to chase the ambulance in his new car.

We watch them drive off. Then Miss Askew tells Cooper,

Elsie, Juna and me to follow her into the staffroom and, between us, we get the story OUT - that Gilby *isn't* the dreamboat most teachers think he is, but a nasty, violent BULLY BOY. Elsie has, what is called EMPIRICAL EVIDENCE* because her ear is already blooming with another Gilby-inflicted bruise.

Miss Askew is distressed. 'For *crying out LOUD*. **WHY** didn't you tell me sooner?' she says, wringing her hands. (That, as they say, is the million-dollar question.) 'And *why* didn't you tell your parents?'

Oh dear. How to answer that one? I have a go at reading my friends' thoughts...

`Cooper:` Well Miss, it's like this - it's best if I keep out of my dad's way...

`Juna:` I don't really talk to my parents, Miss...

`Elsie:` I don't want my mum to be stressed, Miss...

No one speaks. I need to hold hands with someone, but Cooper's next to me and that would be too weird. Cooper touches my hand with his little finger.

I manage to say, 'We wanted to, but it was complicated...'

Miss Askew does her jug impression and fixes me with her button eyes.

I don't know what else to say, so I add, 'We didn't want to spoil your play.'

'***FORGET*** the play!' cries Miss Askew, waving her hands in the air. 'The play is ***NOT*** important. Children's *welfare* is important. *That's* why I'm going to RWANDA!'

Oh, I think. The cat's out of the bag now.

'*Good heavens!*' says Miss Askew. 'What is *wrong* with a school when children are bullied and no one sees it?'

I have no idea how to answer this question. I look at Cooper. He doesn't know either.

Miss Askew sinks onto the staffroom sofa and looks at the floor. 'That is a rhetorical question, addressed to myself,' she says quietly.

I'll look up the word 'rhetorical' later. My knees are shaking. I don't know if Miss Askew is mad at us, at Gilby, or herself – it's hard to tell.

Then she says, 'None of this is your fault. It is the fault of the school. It is the fault of the teachers. It is the fault of a school policy* that isn't clear… I'm *so sorry*.'

Sorry is a good word, but now we have other worries.

Elsie says in a small voice, 'Miss, who will play Charlie?'

'Oh, good grief!' says Miss Askew, sounding defeated. She turns a paler shade of beige and blends in with the paint on the walls. She sighs and stares into space.

'I'll do it, Miss,' says Cooper, quietly. 'I know the songs and I've heard the lines enough times.'

'Can you sing?' asks Miss Askew.

Cooper shrugs. 'No idea,' he says.

Another silence.

Miss Askew smiles and says, 'Cooper Platt... You are *ON!*'

The show must go on

Miss Askew has telephoned our parents. The story of Gilby is out and my parents are really FREAKED OUT. Then Cadence telephones Mum in tears. She can't believe Elsie has been hiding this from her.

'Why didn't you tell us, Ellie?' demands Dad.

'You must *never* keep anything from us again,' cries Mum.

They hug me and each other. It's like a Booton sandwich, with me squished in the middle. It's nice, but there's a dollop of guilt in there, instead of mayonnaise.

Later, Grandma says, 'It wasn't your fault, Ellie. I can see how difficult this has been for you.'

Thank you Grandma! That makes a BIG difference. If life were simple, I would have told Mrs Jago to EXCLUDE Gilby the MOMENT I first clapped eyes on him – but who would have listened? The problem is, some people make life miserable for others *before* something can be done to stop them. It should have been stopped sooner though. In future, I'll trust my instincts more.

Ever since I saw L-I-E flashed from the lighthouse, I've had a hard time telling the absolute truth. Susannah comes to my room and we sit and chat. It's time to be HONEST. I tell

Susannah that I don't want any more guitar lessons. She looks upset and worried.

'Am I a rubbish teacher?' she asks.

'You're brilliant.' I say. 'It's just that I'm not musical and I can't sing for toffee, so it's pointless.'

Susannah tells me that singing comes easily to some people, and others have to work at it – but if music sounds like music – and not a clanging mess, then you *can* learn to sing in tune.

'You enjoy singing, Ellie – please don't stop. Any song, sincerely sung, is beautiful, and you're learning guitar chords really quickly.'

Sharing a worry and being reassured is like a dose of nice-tasting medicine. I feel *so* much better. There's nothing wrong with having to work hard at something, is there?

Susannah tells me she was bullied at school. A group of girls told her she was ugly and they pushed her around. One girl even brought scissors to school and cut her hair. When she told the people at the children's home where she lived, they let her down by not taking it seriously. She felt very alone – but now she has people in her life who are helpful and kind.

Susannah says, 'Bullies are insecure, Ellie. *They* feel worthless – so they want to make others feel worthless. They think this will make them feel better – but it doesn't. They get caught up in a cycle of being mean and nasty. They're setting themselves up for a miserable life.'

I listen. I understand. But I'm not quite ready to feel sorry for Gilby.

Thursday night: the first performance of the play

Body temperature: 37 degrees Celsius (normal)

Energy levels: Super-alert.

Head: Buzzing with bright colours and random lines from the play.

Outlook: Fatalistic yet hopeful.

I stand in the wings with the cast. I'd wish them all good luck by saying, *break a leg,* but there might be another literal thinker in the crowd. Miss Askew hovers. Tonight she's accessorized her beige outfit with a brown scarf.

If anything goes wrong, Miss Askew, Lara Jeffreys and I are supposed to spring into action like ninjas and sort it out. I cross my fingers behind my back and hope that nothing bad will happen.

Mrs Jago goes on stage, taps the microphone, cranks up the volume and launches into her, *WELCOME TO OUR WONDERFUL SCHOOL* speech, where *every* pupil is SPECIAL*, every* teacher is BRILLIANT and *everyone* is SO, SO VERY HAPPY. It's complete overkill, of course. She mentions a *mishap,* resulting in an unfortunate injury and a *resourceful pupil* stepping in to fill the part, which is one way of putting it, I suppose.

'But *that's* what it's all about,' she says chirpily. 'In this school we're a *team* and we all *help* one another to *make things happen!*'

Not quite the truth of course, because sometimes the truth isn't pretty.

Mrs Jago says she's *sure* the audience is in for a *fabulous* evening – so just sit back, relax and enjoy this *marvellous* school play, written and directed by our own *treasured* Miss Askew.

At least that bit is true.

I now understand the PAVAROTTI PRINCIPLE. Even if you're *terrified* of failing – you'll never know if you can succeed at something unless you give it a go. Cooper is clearly TERRIFIED. He has *never* rehearsed this part – or even been in a play before – and he has *no idea* if he can act or sing.

But – he is… GREAT!

I mean – if you make allowances for how nervous he is, and the few lines he fluffs, and when he swings his foot to the right, instead of the left and accidentally kicks Purdy Wallace in the shin, and when his voice doesn't quite reach the high note in the *I'm sorry* song – he really *is* GREAT – and it's *great* to realise that **GREAT doesn't have to mean PERFECT.**

Gilby was a natural villain – but convincing an audience that your character evolves into a good guy, was *way* beyond Gilby's acting ability. Cooper though, makes you *love* Charlie. Who would have thought that possible? You *really want* him to change – and when he does – it's **BRILLIANT!** By the end of the play, everyone is clapping so hard, my ears hurt.

Elsie beams. She holds hands with Cooper and they take their bows. The cast take theirs.

Miss Askew is very, *very,* VERY PLEASED.

Friday's child is loving and giving

I've just found out that Cooper was born on a Friday which means, according to the rhyme, that he's *loving and giving*. I won't argue with that.

Despite Wednesday's child (me) supposedly being *full* of woe, I'm feeling pretty upbeat. Yay!

It's hard to concentrate on schoolwork when it's the end of term and you know there's a play to perform again in the evening.

Cooper is in a daze. He can't quite believe what happened last night. We keep telling him that he was *amazing*, but he's not convinced and he's nervous he's got to do it again tonight *and* twice again tomorrow! It's that pesky problem of *confidence* again.

Elsie seems like Elsie again. She's *so glad* she doesn't have to play opposite Gilby, she keeps doing a little dance. I'll be honest. When she got home last night, she had a good cry. I don't blame her. So did her mum, Cadence. It sort of washed all the sadness and uncertainty away because they promised, *from now on*, they will be open and honest with each other. They're a team – they have to stick together and work things out. So, even though Elsie's ear is bruised –

she's not hiding it – and she's getting a *lot* of sympathy. Most kids are really fed up with Gilby, and although it's not right to be glad that he's in hospital, no one's exactly sad either. I'd be lying if I said there wasn't a *bit* of a celebration. I mean, his leg hasn't fallen off or anything. He will get better. He's just going to have a very different Christmas to the one he thought he was going to have, and it serves him right.

Another thing to celebrate: the bunting idea has WORKED! Cooper, Elsie, Juna and I have lockers *full* of messages for Miss Askew. Everyone is very hush-hush about it – but there are lots of meaningful looks going round the school. In fact, we're getting nods and smiles from kids we've never spoken to before. Juna is a bit freaked out with all the positive attention – but I don't think it will do her any harm.

The Friday performance of the school play

On the *upside* – only a few mishaps: forgotten lines (not many), one lighting problem, (the waifs and strays had to squeeze into one spotlight if they wanted to be seen – it was like a rugby scrum) and Jonathan Goldman's trousers split when he did his cartwheel (very funny - lots of laughter).

Cooper missed the high note, but who cares! Otherwise - *amazing!*

Elsie – completely brilliant!

Rest of cast - fab!

Miss Askew - accessorizing with lavender, no less.

On the downside - Abigail Jennings has started to hang

around Cooper. Not sure he's noticed yet – but she's making it pretty obvious that she likes him again.

Get the flags out!

Saturday morning. I'm sitting at the kitchen table in my pink teddy jammies, munching my way through a bowl of Coco Pops, when the doorbell rings. Grandma goes to see who it is, and then in walks Jack.

I can tell you, it's not the outfit I wanted to be wearing when *he* called round.

Grandma thinks Jack is wonderful. Herman thinks Jack is wonderful. Mum and Dad think he's wonderful. In fact, everyone who meets Jack thinks he's *wonderful*. That's because he is polite, talented and sensible. He's also tall, has a nice smile and clean finger nails.

'Such a thoughtful boy,' says Grandma, if ever his name crops up in conversation.

I'm not convinced he's so thoughtful though – turning up at 8:30 before I've had the chance to put on a pair of jeans and a decent T-shirt, or even brush my hair. *Au naturel*, as they say in France, is *not* my best look.

'*Bonjour,*' I say. '*Quelle surprise.*' For some reason I speak a bit of French when I'm nervous. I pick up Grandma's newspaper and disappear behind it.

I'm sending out *thoughts* to Grandma: NO, I'm *not* being rude. PLEASE get him *out* of here so I can *disappear* and get *dressed!*

Luckily, Grandma is good at reading thoughts.

She says to Jack, 'Would you like to see my latest sculpture?'

Jack, being very polite, says, 'I'd love to.'

They disappear into the workshop.

I put the paper down (Oh no! I was holding it upside down! Maybe he didn't notice?) and make a run for it.

Ten minutes later, I saunter casually into the kitchen wearing my best black jeans and Nike trainers, my pink T-shirt with the wise owl design, and my new indigo hoodie. Almost my favourite outfit... it's only Jack, after all.

Jack sits at the table and tells me he arrived last night on the late train. He's got his camera bag with him, of course. Jack takes photographs *all* the time, so you have to be *very* careful not to pull any monkey faces when he's around, *and* if you want to be remembered for having a fashion sense - dress *wisely.*

I tell Jack about the bunting for Miss Askew.

'Amazing,' says Jack. 'You're intuitive, Ellie.'

I need a definition of *intuitive*, but I'm pretty sure it's a compliment and I start to blush. I drop down on the floor and give Herman a hug, so that I can hide my face in his fur.

Eddie comes in.

Jack stands up and they do this hand clasp, shoulder hug thing that boys do to look cool. I'm surprised Eddie knows it.

'What's going down, man?' asks Eddie.

'The usual,' says Jack.

'Awesome,' says Eddie.

I roll my eyes. I don't understand boy-speak.

I get my jacket and Herman's lead. The plan is this: anyone who wants to help with the bunting should meet outside the Box Brownie at 9:30. Whoever turns up can come to my house – and we'll sit at the kitchen table and fix the bunting together. All this has been whispered between *trusted people*, and who knows *how* it will turn out?

I pop my head round the door and say, 'I'm going to meet Elsie. I'll give Herman a run on the beach first.'

Eddie and Jack are talking football - another language I don't understand.

Jack says, 'I'll come with you, Ellie.'

'Oh, all right,' I say, feeling colour creeping into my cheeks again.

Eddie laughs and I give him a dirty look.

We walk down the hill towards the beach. Jack is full of questions about Gilby, the play and the lighthouse code. There's so much to tell him. He's pretty shocked that my parents found out about the bullying only *two* days ago, when Mrs Jago phoned them with all the gory details. He stops in his tracks and looks at me.

'Don't give me a hard time,' I tell him. 'Believe me, if anything like this happens again, I'll be the first in line to tell.'

I tell Jack about Gilby pushing Elsie into the curtain and how he got tangled up with Cooper and launched himself off the stage like a baby bird expecting to fly. Jack is completely *amazed* that quiet, insecure Cooper volunteered and is now the *leading boy* in the play. So the saying – *you can't count on any man* – ISN'T TRUE at all! I'm proud of Cooper. My first impression of him was *not good*. It just goes to show that sometimes, people can surprise you.

I tell Jack who was behind the lighthouse code and that the letters spell out: **Good luck Miss Askew**.

He pulls a face and says, 'That's pretty lame.'

I nod. It was probably Dad's idea and I suddenly feel very sorry for him. Last night I heard Mum and Dad talking in the den, so I pressed my ear to the door to make sure Mum was OK. But it was Dad who sounded upset. I mean, he's a pain, but it turns out he's been very worried about his book.

He said, 'I've put my heart into this, Flora. It might even sell, who knows? Then, at last, I can say that I'm providing for my family. I'm an average writer and a less than average husband. You deserve so much more. I'm frightened of losing you.'

I heard Mum say, 'You always put your heart into your work, Walter. I've always believed in your ability. But there's more to life than work. I need you to put your heart into our marriage as well. Money's tight, but we always get by. We're a team. We can support one another. You forget that, sometimes. It makes me feel invisible.'

I never knew that money was tight and that Dad thinks he's a less than average husband. I never knew that Mum felt invisible. Why is life so complicated?

I think it took a lot for Dad to admit he was frightened – but at least he told someone. My parents can help one another. It's difficult deciding *who* you should tell when something is worrying you – but the main thing is, you should TELL SOMEONE who can help you.

Jack says, 'You're quiet, Ellie.'

'Sorry,' I say.

And that's another thing I've realised. Just because someone is quiet (like Juna) doesn't mean there's nothing going on in their brain. Brains are funny things. Well, not funny, ha ha. If you've ever seen a picture of a brain, they're yucky and not funny at all. Brains find solutions to problems and questions. If it's something simple like 2 + 2, *everyone's* brain will come up with the same answer. But if it's complicated and especially if it's about *people*, there are lots of solutions. Gilby's answer to the question: *How should I treat people?* is *Hurt and threaten them.* His solution is WRONG and NOT GOOD. He's not *problem solving* at all. In fact, he creates problems for people, including himself. Not only does he have a broken leg, but he might be excluded from school - and no one I know has rushed to send him a get-well card.

Some brains come up with solutions that are HALF RIGHT and NOT BAD. The solution to the lighthouse code: **Good luck Miss Askew**, isn't *bad,* it's just sort of... *not enough*.

And sometimes - just sometimes – there's a solution that's PERFECT for everyone, but I don't think that happens very often.

I just want to get it right for Miss Askew. OK - she gets stressed and she is a bit beige. Some kids call her, *The Beigen* - but she's definitely *not* boring. She really wants to help kids and she puts her heart into everything she does. I've not known her for long, but I will *miss* her.

Jack stands in front of me.

'Are you all right, Ellie?' he says. 'You look like you're going to cry.'

I swallow hard. 'I'm fine,' I say. 'It's just the wind in my eyes.'

The air is full of noise. Seagulls circle and screech. Waves hammer the beach. I start to run.

'Come on!' I yell to Jack.

The tide is out and the sand is smooth and firm. Jack runs and cruises past. I sprint and almost catch him - then we start to laugh. We get to the other side of the cove. I stop to catch my breath but Jack runs in circles with his arms out like a plane. He's not bothered what he looks like! Herman runs with him, wagging his tail, splashing, barking and bouncing. Herman lives in the moment. He is a very wise dog.

We turn to walk back. I ask Jack lots of questions about his school, his friends, his photography. He's a very interesting boy. I don't tell him about Juna's countdown posters though. That story is on a strictly need-to-know basis.

When we come up the slipway, outside the Box Brownie café there's a crowd including Elsie, Juna and Cooper. Believe it or not – mixed in with all the nice kids, is Abigail Jennings.

I smile. I'll give her a chance. Like Susannah says, bullies want others to feel worthless because they feel worthless themselves – and they're setting themselves up for a miserable life. It would be sad if Abigail had a lifetime of misery ahead of her.

So Juna, Cooper, Elsie, Purdy, Cody, Thomas, Madeleine, Frankie, Abigail, Kit, Laurel, Flix, Alfie, Zara, Daniel, Jack and I sit round the kitchen table punching holes in pieces of plastic paper. One flag is cut into the shape of Miss Askew's glasses, which she wears on a chain round her neck.

Grandma, Mum, Nanna, Gramps and Cadence, help us too. Then *love-rival* Maggie turns up. I hold my breath.

Jem must have fixed everything because Cadence says, 'Sorry for even *thinking* you were Jem's type. Can I have a hug?' and they fall into one another's arms, laughing their heads off.

Elsie and I look at one another and shrug. Who knows what adults think sometimes?

Cadence puts a plate of cookies on the table, and there's Grandma's cake (chocolate and lemon drizzle) and bags of crisps from Jem's grocery store. It's not exactly a health-fest, but you can't be sensible all the time. Everyone is chatting and laughing, and Herman is so HAPPY. Most dogs are very clever. They don't waste time being unfriendly – they just live their lives and make lots of friends along the way.

By the time we've finished stringing the bunting, we realise we've got enough to go round the Box Brownie café and more besides. It's so much more than **GOOD LUCK, MISS ASKEW**. There are thank you notes, memories, jokes, good luck messages and drawings. All mini works of art.

Gramps chuckles and whispers to Juna and me, 'By the

time Miss Askew has finished reading all these messages, she'll be smacking her gums together like Nanna.'

I'm not sure that's a kind thought because Nanna wears false teeth – but it is quite funny.

'What are you laughing at?' sniffs Nanna.

Gramps winks at us. 'Just a bit of nonsense, my dear,' he says.

Dad, Jem and Eddie are at the Box Brownie café, getting it ready for the party tonight. Susannah is with them, thank goodness. She'll keep them on track. They're planning a surprise, I think. My guess is that Susannah might sing a few songs. I hope so. Miss Askew will *love* that.

Hitting a high note

Saturday evening: the last performance of the play. I sit next to Mum, who sits next to Dad, who jiggles Fin on his knee. Cadence and Jem sit on the row in front holding hands. Grandma, Nanna and Gramps sit on the row behind. Eddie and Susannah are doing something secret at the Box Brownie – but I'm not worried. Some secrets are good.

Jack is allowed to wander round, because he's the official photographer, assisted by Maggie who carries his equipment. They skulk around in the dark, dressed in black so people don't notice them. I do though. It's great seeing Jack with a grown-up assistant. I feel like laughing, but I don't, especially when the waifs and strays are singing their sad songs.

The spotlight follows Elsie around the stage. Her hair is loose and sparks in the light, and she's perfectly calm singing really high notes. It's a pure sound that sails through the air, touches your skin and makes you shiver.

Dad whispers, 'She's a star!'

Mum nods happily. It's strange staring at someone in the dark, when they don't even know you're looking at them. I want to always have a picture in my head of my mum smiling. She's so pretty and for now, at least, she is living in the moment. The music – the singing – sitting next to Dad, Fin and me – makes her happy.

I lean forward and look at Dad. He's nodding his head in time to the music. His teeth stick out and his nose is a bit on the big side, like his African elephant ears. But that's my dad and his face couldn't be nicer. Fin is still, his eyes like saucers. Tonight he's sweet.

When Cooper comes on stage, Fin shouts, 'It's Cooper!' and the audience chuckles.

Did Cooper hit his high note? Not quite, but when he sings his *I'm sorry* song, a tear trickles down my cheek and I think: *NO!* I understand why Miss Askew doesn't like showing emotion in public. I don't want to look wrung out like a damp cloth when the lights go up.

I sniff as quietly as I can. Mum pokes me in the ribs. She stuffs a tissue in my hand and I see she's crying too. We smile at one another.

Elsie and Cooper hold hands. All the cast come on stage and sing the *Happy Ever After* song. Juna holds hands with Madeleine and Erin. I've never seen them hold hands before. They take a bow.

And then, it's over to us.

We clap. *And clap.* **And clap. AND CLAP.** My hands feel like they'll drop off, but I *can't* stop clapping! Fin stands on Dad's knee and claps.

He shouts, 'Cooper! Elsie! Juna! Hello!'

Cooper spots him and waves and Fin laughs his head off.

Elsie waves at me.

Oh, I've just noticed. I'm standing up and shouting,

'*THAT WAS BRILLIANT!*' How embarrassing! When you live in the moment, sometimes you don't really know what you're doing!

Mum cheers. Dad whistles.

Grandma leans over and squeezes my shoulder. 'Pure joy,' she says, laughing.

Mrs Jago comes on stage to finish off her *'This school is wonderful'* speech – but at least, tonight, she's telling the truth.

'The play was AWESOME!' (Yes, Mrs Jago uses the word, *awesome.*) 'And what can I say about Miss Askew?' she says with a little tremble in her voice. 'She has tirelessly supported our school for *so many* years. There will be parents in the audience who were taught by her' - some murmur and flutter their hands in the air - 'and no doubt, some will have starred in one of Miss Askew's plays.' More flutters. 'Because children *do* become stars under Miss Askew's direction and tonight, I'm sure you'll agree, we saw these young people *shine* like stars – and that's because they have been encouraged and cared for by a *wonderful* teacher... Miss Askew, please join me.'

Miss Askew steps into the spotlight. My mouth drops open. She's wearing pink!

Everyone claps and claps. Then there's a hush - because Mrs Jago becomes a bit teary. She dabs at her eyes.

She says, 'Oh bother! I should be used to this. I've seen colleagues come and go over the years. We're happy to be a team and we're sad when one of us leaves – but we always wish each other well. But colleagues become friends, as dear to us as our own family – sometimes a lot *dearer*.' The audience chuckles. 'As you will probably know, Miss Askew is leaving our school. What you might *not* know is that she's going far away to Rwanda, a country with a troubled past.' There are gasps of surprise. It *has* been a well kept secret after all! Miss Askew clasps her hands tightly and stares at the floor. '*Every* child deserves the best of care and children who are troubled deserve it even more. It takes a brave, wonderful and dedicated teacher to take on such challenging work. I know you will all join me in wishing Miss Askew *good luck*.'

And I suddenly understand. *Good luck* is a short and simple message – but when it's said with love, it means a lot. Mrs Jago opens her mouth to say more, but nothing comes out. She dabs her eyes again, then hugs Miss Askew.

Everyone claps really hard. **NOISE!** Lots of hoots and whistles and shouts. The biggest bunch of flowers gets launched across the stage into Miss Askew's arms. I'm not sure what I shout. I'm laughing *and* crying – but I don't care. I'm living in the moment!

The moon is out. It's a cold, clear night. Our footsteps echo as we march down the promenade to the Box Brownie café. There's chatter and our breath hangs in the air.

Miss Askew notices the bunting strung outside the café, flapping in the breeze.

'How festive!' she says happily.

The café doors are open and folded back. There are patio heaters, candles flickering in jars and lots of twinkle lights.

Now, at the end of an ordeal, good or bad – a nice quiet chat and a cup of tea is a good way of making sense of it all. But this isn't one of those times.

'Let's pop some bubbly!' somebody shouts.

Everyone cheers.

There's a little stage area with a microphone on a stand (you see, I'm right – Susannah *is* going to sing) and a clear space (for dancing, I guess) and clusters of tables and chairs.

Cadence goes behind the microphone. She taps it and says nervously, 'Testing, testing.'

There's a hush.

'Welcome to the Box Brownie café, everyone. The play was *magnificent*, and the leading lady was *divine* -' she says, pulling Elsie to her '- and I'm *not* saying that just because she's my peachy little kid!' There are cheers and laughter.

Elsie forces a smile but looks a bit mortified. I know *exactly* what she's thinking: PARENTS CAN BE *SO* EMBARASSING!

'And tonight,' says Cadence, 'we're here, not only to celebrate the fabulous school play and the brilliant cast, but to honour Miss Askew, who is a *wonderful* teacher and a very dear member of our community.' Cadence beckons to Miss Askew who steps into the limelight and goes as pink as her jumper. She has *colour!* 'You're a wonderful woman, Dorothy, and we love you,' laughs Cadence and hugs her.

Everyone laughs, even Miss Askew, and there's another round of applause. My hands are starting to hurt!

'We have music. We have food. And you're right - we even have champagne!' cries Cadence. Everyone cheers.

'But that's just for the grown-ups,' she laughs.

The kids chorus, 'Aww.'

'So, let's enjoy the moment,' she says. 'LET'S PARTY!'

And right on cue, music fills the air and the grown-ups and a few brave kids start to throw some shapes - I wouldn't call it dancing exactly.

Jack comes over to us with his camera. Cooper stretches his arms around Elsie, Juna and me.

'After three,' says Cooper. 'One, two, three…'

We all cry, *'Cheese!'*

Jack captures the moment. He hands his camera to Elsie and stands by me.

'You know what you've got to do,' he says, smiling.

I think I do. I'm starting to read Jack's thoughts too.

'After three?' I say.

Jack nods.

'One, two, *three*!'

And we both pull BIG MONKEY FACES.

'That's one for the album,' laughs Cooper.

Then Susannah plays her guitar and sings some songs. Everyone sways to the music, even those who are balancing plates full of nibbles.

I notice Herman trotting round. He's a very sociable dog and knows how to mingle. Suddenly, he wags his tail and runs down the promenade into the night. A few moments later he reappears, looking *very* pleased with himself because he's with… THE WATFORD WARBLER - who just happens to be a HUGE favourite of Miss Askew's. *Everyone* seems to know who he is. Who would have thought it?

Dad's pretty chuffed, especially when The Warbler takes the microphone and says that my dad's book will make him famous, *at last* - ha, ha, ha.

'This is a very special night,' says The Warbler, and he talks about Miss Askew, as though he's known her all his life. Dad has briefed him well. Then he sings and casts an eternal anti-beige spell on her. I never thought I'd see Miss Askew looking so excited and girlie.

Worse is to come!

The Warbler looks at Mum and says, 'And this one's for you, Flora,' and he starts to warble his way through a mushy song called *Lady In Red.** You probably won't know it. It's ancient. It's the song my mum and dad fell in *lurve* to.

So, Mum, who's wearing her best *red* dress slow dances with Dad, with everyone watching. Honestly, there are some things a kid shouldn't see – and this is one of them. (Only joking – I'm glad they're happy.)

Jem tops up Miss Askew's glass. She sits down next to a patio heater and looks merry. A piece of bunting comes loose and wafts past her head. She catches it... and then she looks at it…

She starts to read the flags that have been flapping above her head all night. Her hand flutters to her lips.

Oh no! Please don't cry!

She looks up and spots me. I hold my breath. Is she angry? No.

She smiles, does her jug impression and mouths, 'Did *you* do this?'

I smile and shrug. It wasn't me, after all. It was

EVERYONE.

Jem and Eddie disappear in the direction of the lighthouse. I know what's coming next. Then Maggie, laughing her head off as usual, grabs the microphone and announces there are fireworks. Oh well, that's a surprise! She points in the direction of the lighthouse and everyone lines up. Fireworks are always good. And while we are watching the fireworks, the red letters start to flash.

G-O-O-D -- L-U-C-K – M-I-S-S – A-S-K-E-W

The Warbler puts his arm round her. She laughs and someone shouts: 'Three cheers for Miss Askew. Hip, hip -' and we all shout: 'HURRAY!'

'Hip, hip!'
'HURRAY!'
'Hip, hip!'
'HURRAY!'

VERY LATE SATURDAY NIGHT (or very early Sunday morning)

Would you believe it – the Watford Warbler is snoring away in our spare bedroom and I'll have to have breakfast with him in the morning. I hope he doesn't ask if I'm a fan. That might be a tad awkward!

Still, after that I'm meeting *some* of my friends - Elsie, Cooper, Juna, Jack, Flix, Cody and Frankie. We're going to the cinema together, but first we'll take the bunting down and put it in a box. It's heavy, so we'll post it to Miss Askew when she goes to Rwanda. She told us she will put it round her new classroom. She was pretty happy about it. She cried – but what's a few tears between friends? She won't forget us.

Do you know – I've just had a thought... I don't like being called Smelly Boots. It's not nice when people call you something that's not respectful. From now on, when I mention the opera singer, I'll use his proper name. After all, I wouldn't call him *The Watford Warbler* to his face.

I curl up on my window seat. Herman puts his head in my lap and says goodnight. He's a tired dog. The lighthouse beam sweeps round. No red letters tonight. That's all done with.

Except... what happened to the I LOVE YOU* message? Who's that for, I wonder? I guess I'll have to wait to find out. I sigh. There's always another puzzle to solve.

Stars twinkle their old light. I'm not looking into the past though. Life is now and tonight, I'm happy.

I climb into bed and listen to the wind and to Herman quietly snoring...

Goodnight, sleep tight

Ellie x

Extra Jots...

*Pavarotti

Luciano Pavarotti was born on the 12 October 1935, in Italy. Luciano liked singing, but he loved football more and wanted to be a goalkeeper. His mum wasn't keen on this career choice and thought he should be a teacher. In the end, even though his parents were against it, he gave *singing* a go and discovered he was the best opera singer in the world! I hope his parents apologised for interfering in his life. He died on the 6 September 2007, aged 71.

*Over The Rainbow

I first heard this song when I watched the film, *The Wizard of Oz*, with Grandma. It's about a girl called Dorothy who carries around a little dog called Toto. Grandma once had a dog like Toto, though Herman is our dog now, and only a weightlifter would be able to carry him around.

The tune was written ages ago, in 1939, by Harold Arlen. The lyrics are by E.Y. Harburg. Dorothy is looking for a place where there's no trouble and she thinks this place is somewhere over the rainbow. She's right. No matter where you are – you can always find a bit of trouble.

*Ernie Wise

Ernie was best friends with Eric. They met when they were young and decided to work together making people laugh. They had to work *really* hard to get good at their job (the Pavarotti principle) but in the end, they were simply the BEST. Their act was known as Morecambe and Wise and you can still watch their shows on TV, usually at Christmas. We all watch it in the den and *laugh our heads off*. It's sad they're no longer alive – but Grandma says, wherever they are now, they're still making people laugh.

*a loan shark

Most people have to borrow money at sometime in their lives. If you borrow money to buy a house, it's called a mortgage and you usually get the money from a bank or a building society. But there are lots of people who lend money and not all of these people are good or fair.

A very simple example: if you borrow £100, a bank would expect you to pay back £100, plus a bit extra, to make it worth their while. The extra is called interest. A LOAN SHARK will charge a VERY HIGH INTEREST – much more than is reasonable. And that's why they're called SHARKS because they are *cold, greedy and completely ruthless* and they might as well bite people's hands off when they loan them money. Swim clear of loan sharks!

*idioms and literal thinking

Dad likes explaining things like metaphors, idioms and similes. How I understand it - an idiom is a thing you say with a FIGURATIVE meaning, which is different from a LITERAL meaning. A good example of this is when theatre folk say *break a leg* (which is FIGURATIVE and means good luck) because the LITERAL meaning will result in hospitals overcrowded with actors on crutches.

So when Mum said, 'Get off your high horse,' (a *figurative idiom*) she didn't *actually* mean it, because Dad has never been on a horse in his life. She just meant that he was being a bit too self-important.

*'The lady doth protest too much'

This comes from Dad's favourite Shakespeare play, *Hamlet*. Shakespeare lived a *l-o-n-g* time ago and wrote plays with a quill, which is a feather dipped in ink. If he were alive today, he would have his own drama channel and Dad would watch all his shows, probably on Sky TV.

*PHATIC communication

This is chit-chat or small talk. It's the sort of thing you say to be friendly and fill in a bit of space. When you call, '*Hi, how are you?*' to someone across the street, you would expect them to say, '*Fine thanks,*' and not stop traffic to give you an hour's worth of their woes and worries.

*Rwanda

Rwanda is a beautiful country in Africa with rolling hills, grassy plains and mountains, where mountain gorillas live. It is also a country with a very violent past. There are two main groups of people who live there: the Tutsi people and the

Hutu people. At times their problems have been so bad there has been lots of killing. When TERRIBLE things like this happen, the people who've experienced it can be upset and hurt for the rest of their lives. The children of Rwanda have a good chance of living happily, if they are helped and supported by education and kindness. In Rwanda, there's a shortage of schools and teachers, which isn't fair – so when someone like Miss Askew offers to help out, it's another step in the right direction.

*swan song

People in ancient Greece believed that a swan could sing a beautiful song as it died. That's a bit sad and actually, swans can't sing for toffee - but what it means is that if you're at the end of anything, it's best to go out on a happy note so that people remember you in a good way. The school play isn't Miss Askew's swan song though. She's not at the end of her life – just at the end of her time at our school – and her whole career as a teacher has been a big success and it's not over. Kids of Rwanda – brace yourselves!

*'This is the way the world ends. Not with a bang, but a whimper.'

This is from the poem, The Hollow Men, written in 1925 by T. S. Eliot when he was going through a difficult, glass half-empty phase of his life. He did, eventually, feel more positive about life and wrote some happy poems, which is good to know.

*cherry on the parfait

A parfait is a French dessert with whipped cream, eggs and fruit – and if you pop a cherry on the top, it looks perfect. *Parfait* is French for *perfect*. When I said this, I was being **sarcastic** because when we saw Jem with Maggie, who we thought was his new girlfriend (she isn't, thank goodness) – it topped off a *perfectly* AWFUL day.

*Wednesday's child is full of woe

Well – if you tell a kid that, it's not going to set them up for a very happy life, is it? This is how the rhyme goes:

Monday's child is fair of face

(Good looking and knows it)

Tuesday's child is full of grace

(Gets into trouble and worms their way out of it)

Wednesday's child is full of woe

(A bit of a drama queen)

Thursday's child has far to go

(Doesn't learn from their mistakes)

Friday's child is loving and giving

(Normalish)

Saturday's child works hard for his living

(Needs to lighten up)

But the child who is born on Sunday is bonny and blithe and good and gay

(Perfect but probably a bit boring)

Of any day, I think I'd want to be born on a Friday. Thankfully though, the rhyme isn't true.

*auras

Susannah says people have an energy that you can almost see. If your energy is good and kind, the colour of it will be bright and lovely – but if your energy is bad, people will sense a darkness about you. It's hard to explain and some people don't think auras exist. (Dad doesn't.) I'm not sure myself, but when I see Gilby, he seems dull and grey, though Elsie's smile is so bright, it can light up a room. Maybe that's why they say, if you're depressed or down, you're blue?

*Queen Victoria

Queen Victoria was a Monday's child (fair of face) and lived for 81 years and 7 months. She became Queen of Great Britain and Ireland when she was only eighteen years old. Victoria didn't quite get along with her mum and hardly ever saw her dad, so she was a pretty lonely kid. When she was twenty-one, she married Prince Albert, her German cousin. It doesn't sound like a good idea to me, but she was very keen on him, so her life bucked up a lot. They had nine children, though she wasn't always thrilled about that. She was younger than my mum when her husband died. The sadness made her depressed for a long time, and she wore black for the rest of her life.

*empirical evidence

This is evidence that you can actually *show* to people and so, when you want to prove a point, it comes in very handy.

School policy - sounds boring but it's vital

In the UK, every state school *must* have an anti-bullying policy to encourage good behaviour and prevent all forms of bullying. At the moment it's up to each state school to decide what sort of policy they will have and how much they will publicise it, so some schools might take it more seriously than others. Private schools (which aren't free – you have to pay to be educated there) are not even required to have an anti-bullying policy, which to me, is WRONG and *VERY WORRYING*.

Jack's school, for example, has a TELLING POLICY, which means that *everyone* in the school is *responsible* for telling a teacher if they see bullying going on. *Every pupil* knows this, so does *every parent or guardian* – and they are reminded of it often, **so no one FORGETS.** If your school has got it right, it should be CLEAR TO EVERYONE that **bullying is just PLAIN WRONG** and that *everyone* has a responsibility to PREVENT it from happening in the first place.

But one thing's for sure – *if you're being bullied*, you should TELL SOMEONE who will LISTEN and be prepared to HELP you.

Lady In Red

This is a mushy song you can only slow dance to. It's by a singer-songwriter called Chris de Burgh who first sang it in the summer of 1986, the year my parents met one another.

This song was playing when Dad asked a pretty girl wearing a red dress to dance. That was my mum and they've been stuck with one another ever since.

*more about Juna's doodles

Feelings somehow find a way to express themselves. When Juna was unhappy, all her drawings were bleak. I spotted the countdown code in her doodles of sad and scared faces. Without even knowing it, she was trying to communicate how frightened and upset she was. In her doodles on page 145, I saw 2F (left face) and 1A (right face).

The doodles above show 6-A and 5-C. Just look at the eye area. The doodle on page 128 is 3-O.

Yesterday, when she was going home, Juna gave me a drawing of a cute teddy bear. I guess she's feeling a whole lot happier now, and what's even better than that - we're friends.

CUL8R
Juna xx

*the I LOVE YOU files

The only person Eddie loves - apart from his family and friends, and Herman and our cat, Eliza - is Susannah, but I don't think he's told her yet. He really should. That's my opinion anyway.

If anything happens, I'll let you know.